FIELDS OF FIRE

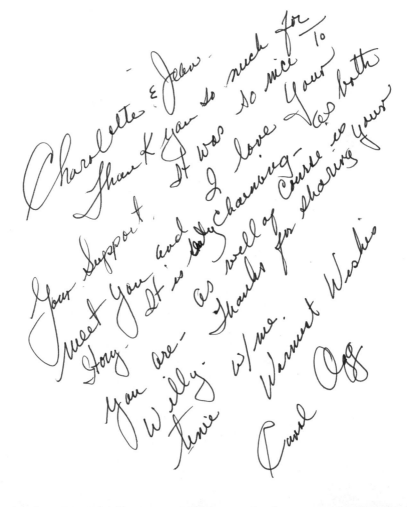

Charolette & Helen -
Thank you so much for
your support. It was so nice to
meet you and I love your
story. It is so very charming - as both
you are - As well of course so
Willy. Thanks for sharing your
Tenie w/ me. Warmest Wishes
Carol Off

FIELDS OF FIRE

CAROL OGG

To order additional copies of this book, contact:
Xlibris Corporation
1-888-795-4274
www.Xlibris.com
Orders@Xlibris.com
20090

Contents

Dedication and Acknowledgements

For my Mom who taught me strength of character; for my dear friend Uschi who endured while I wrote it; for my mentor and friend Kathy who helped me put it all together; for Carole who helped me sort stuff out. A special thanks to Lorraine who helped me find the little things and finally for Struppi and O'fer, my furry friends who played with me when I got tired of working on this.

Disclaimer

This book is a work of fiction. Names, characters, some places, and some incidents either are the product of my imagination or are used fictitiously; and any resemblance to actual persons, living or dead is entirely coincidental.

CHAPTER 1

Handful of Seeds

This is my first visit since Mom died. Her grave looks well manicured. The stone of rose-colored granite glistens in the early spring morning.

"Spring, your favorite time, huh, Mom?" She loved the different color of iris blooming in the garden. The one flower we seemed to have luck at growing. Her first name is an initial carved on the stone, just below the lettering of the last name. She did not use her first name; she didn't like it. Henrietta. She went by Ruth. Born October 1920, died May 1965. Beside her name, space has been left for Dad's name to be carved—or mine.

There is no mention of Robert Glen, the brother I never knew, whose ashes were neatly packed beside her. Big brother Chris thought it best to leave his name off.

"I'm going to Vietnam, Mom," I speak out loud as I sit down close to the edge of her grave. "What do you think of that?"

The wind gives no answer. I sit for a while and then quietly leave the cemetery to make a short swing out to Sand Draw.

It's in the middle of nowhere; a dusty little settlement called Sand Draw, Wyoming. It's like someone took a handful of seeds and threw them on the ground—hard.

The green framed house that loomed before me as a child still stands there. With a cold shudder, I turn toward the west and gaze at the skeletal remains of the Meszkat's trailer. Glad that he is dead, but even so fear zooms through me like cold ice against a front tooth.

The fence to the sheep pen still stands; the cement foundation to the barn is all that is left. The smell burns my nostrils as I fight back the memories.

Peanuts' back is very wide; it's like sitting on the floor.

"Ms. Annie," I hear Mom call me from the front porch. "You ride that horse up here before you go anywhere else . . . right now!"

I am trying to kick Peanuts' side so that he will move faster. "I'm coming, Mom," I holler back.

Peanuts begin to do a stiff-legged trot, and I am bouncing up and down like I'm on a trampoline. I grab the tuft of hair just at the beginning of his mane.

I see Mom walk down off the porch. Her dark auburn hair blowing in the eternal winds of Wyoming, her hand automatically goes to her forehead to brush aside the unruly result. She is stopping in front of me.

I look down at Mom, and she smiles back. As she reaches up and puts her hand on my knee, I hear her say, "Ya got your lunch?" I nod.

"And where are you goin' on your journey today and who are you?"

"Aw, Mom, I'm just Gail Ann; and me and Peanuts are going over to the bottom of Gas Hill." I point directly in front of me.

"There are sheepherders over there, you know?"

"Ya, I know."

"What have I told you about those sheepherders?"

"You told me not to go hangin' around them. It's no place for little girls."

"Just you remember that, I'll be very mad if I find out you went over there. Promise me you won't go?"

"They're just old sheepherders, Mom."

"Ms. Annie," I hear her raise her voice, "those men aren't anyplace for a little girl to be hanging around. "They are dirty and nasty."

"Aw, Mom, I like to watch them dogs they got and all the little lambs," I whine.

"If I catch you over there, you won't ever get to ride Peanuts again."

Horny toads have this amazing ability to look in two different directions at once. They hurry from bush to bush, sometimes darting over the dry and parched earth, continually searching. Suddenly, it stops, the eyes appear to cross and wham! Its tongue darts in a flash, its mouth cavity looks all gooey and sticky like yellow slime. Its mouth goes closed and occasionally the delicate wings of an insect flutter on the edge of the creature's lips.

The dry gulch affords me the best opportunity to watch the ugly little horny toad scamper along the cliff's edge. Standing on the bottom of the dry gulch, my eyes are level with the ground. Sometimes I forget as I watch him—or maybe it's a her, I don't know the difference, and I get a mouthful of dirt. It's as big as a silver dollar with wrinkles around its neck, a short stubby little tail and colors of varying shades of pale sand. Spiny little growths like stalagmites come out from its head and over its body.

My brother Chris once watched me as I picked up a horny toad, and as he waited he said, "You'll get warts from pickin' up that thing."

I dropped the little toad like a hot potato.

Laughing, he picked up the big rock and casually let it fall on the scampering creature.

Now I move quickly along the dry bed of the gulch as the little creature runs then stops. One eye always seems to be on me. I haven't told anybody about this place. The toad and I can run a long way.

The toad stops; both eyes move upward. It turns toward me, and we are face to face. It freezes. I freeze. Beside the toad is the toe of a boot. I look up.

"What're you doing here, Gail Ann?" Mr. Meszkat asks.

"Boy, Mr. Meszkat, you scared me."

He jumps down beside me into the dry gulch bed. "Your mom know you're way out here?"

I shake my head. The smell of the half-chewed cigar fills my nose.

"What are you doing?" he repeats. I quickly glance to see if the creature has run away. He has.

"Playing Indian," I answer. "Hiding from the cowboys."

"You better get home before"—the yellow stained teeth show through the same yellowish-colored lips—"something happens to you." He grins.

I run. Hard. I look for Peanuts grazing nearby. On the second try, I pull myself up on Peanuts' back and we make off for home, down the pipeline road.

The Jeep is up on blocks and Dad is under the front end, his feet sticking out. I sit quietly waiting and hoping he will want something.

I have carefully watched the boys hand Dad different tools. I have drawn each tool repeatedly, committed their shapes to memory, and I know for what purpose they are used.

Clatter! Clink! Grunts and groans come from under the Jeep. The boys are not here so maybe I can help. Maybe I can be the one who brings him the right tool.

The creeper rolls easily from under the Jeep as Dad pushes his way clear of the running board. He glances and sees me sitting near by.

I smile. He gives no reaction. He gets up and goes to the tool bench.

"I'll help," I offer.

"No place for a girl," he grumbles. "Go help your mother."

"Hi, Mr. Meszkat. Can I come and watch ya today?" I ask, "Grandma Meszkat says you were out here fixin' lamb tails." He is standing in the lambs' pen. Between his legs he has a little lamb. The lamb is bleating and struggling to get free. He has a piece of string in his mouth. He reaches down and takes the long tail of the lamb and holds it with one hand, with the other hand he takes the string from his mouth and twists it round and round the upper portion near the base of the tail. He pulls the string tight and makes a knot. The lamb is free. It runs to the others.

"How come you do that, Mr. Meszkat?"

He looks at me and smiles. "Well, one day I'll come out here and the lamb won't have a tail anymore."

The silver water tank, a stone's throw from the house, is like my watchtower. As I climb on the ladder I can see everywhere around the yard. I look in the distance to where Old Mr. Meszkat has his chickens and turkeys. He has only one turkey now, but I haven't seen it for a while.

I carefully climb down the ladder and head out for the barn. No turkey. I open the barn door. It's as dark as the inside of a cow. I go straight in, whistling or more like blowing air between half-parted lips and now my eyes can see in the dim light.

Mr. Meszkat is standing in the middle of the sheep pen. I see a knife in his hand—his pocketknife, the one he always sharpens.

In the center of the sheep pen hanging by his feet from one of the boards is Tom the turkey. His big wings are spread wide open like he does when he is hot, only this time he is upside down.

"How come ya got Tom hanging there, Mr. Meszkat?" My eyes dart around the barn.

He kneels down before me and looks me right in the eye, and I hear him say, "Tom made me very sad; he told a secret."

My heart feels like it will jump out of my chest.

I see him put the knife in his pocket.

"Aw, Mr. Meszkat, Tom can't talk," I hear myself say. "How can he tell a secret?"

"Ohhh, he can talk, you just have to listen." He moves closer to me. "And since he told my secret, he has to be punished," he whispers right in my ear.

I smell his tobaccoy mouth. It does not smell good. I start to run away. Mr. Meszkat grabs me and swings me in the air as he stands up. He forces my legs so that they are around his middle. His arms hold me against him. I can't move.

"Give old Mr. Meszkat a hug," he says. I put my cheek against his cheek and my arms around his neck and squeeze. I don't like his face; it scratches. He turns his face toward me. I want down.

"Please let me down."

I am squirming trying to get down. He takes his hand and puts it on the back of my head and makes me turn my face toward his face. He puts his mouth on my mouth. It's all wet like my lamb Cotton's mouth gets when she drinks from the bottle.

He stops. He is putting me down. As my feet touch the ground, I hear him say, "That's our secret, huh, Gail Ann."

He still has my hand. I try to get away. He reaches into his pocket and gets out the knife. While holding my hand, he opens the knife.

"Now we have to punish Tom," he says.

I see him take the knife and put it in Tom's mouth. It looks like Tom has eaten it. I see blood running all over Mr. Meszkat's hand. It goes all over the ground in the pen. Tom's wings start flapping like he does when he wants to fly; his mouth opens and closes like he is talking.

I don't hear anything.

There are mountains on the high plains of Wyoming. Those mountains that are covered with sage brush, grease wood bushes, and sometimes scrub pine and birch trees always remind me of the rubber door stops that Mom uses to keep the doors from closing in the house. Sometimes the mountains are purple, sometimes they are a fiery red, and sometimes they are the color of the horny toads, soft sandy.

The mountains are lined up in some places side by side and make perfect valleys to camp. The tops are natural prairie ledges where you can stand and see for miles.

I get Francis, a newly acquired mule Dad had bought for packing out the carcasses shot by rich Easterners during Wyoming's well-known "One Shot Antelope Hunt."

My brother Samuel takes Peanuts.

"Gail Ann, you stay with Samuel and don't go wandering off," Mom says.

"I won't," I promise.

I pull Francis over to the highest part of the wood porch and jumping as hard as I can, I flop over his back like a sack of feed and then swing my right leg over his sway back. Righting myself, I grab hold of the reins that I have tied together, grab the tuft of hair on his mane, and proceed toward the mountains following Samuel.

The sheep wagon is parked just below the ledge of a small rock overhang. They look a lot like Conestoga wagons, except when you open the door, it is a living space neatly configured for maximum use—a table, a bed with storage space underneath, and several shelves.

A kerosene lantern hangs in the middle of the wagon. There are six windows, sometimes they have curtains, usually red checkered ones, sometimes not.

As Samuel and I approach the sheep wagon, we can see the sheepherder off to the right, mounted on his horse, waving to us. We wave back.

I kick Francis, but he does not move any faster. Samuel gallops on toward the sheepherder and the flock.

As I approach them, I watch the dogs lying in wait on their haunches for a wandering lamb or ewe or buck. Those dogs are lightning fast and seem to know when one of them sheep is going to bolt. As soon as the dog has taken care of the strays, he resumes his watch on his haunches. Sometimes a piercing whistle fills the airways as the sheepherder signals the dogs to move the sheep out, to higher ground, the watering hole or maybe better fields.

The dogs begin to weave and dance around the sheep, and the masses begin to move.

Samuel and I stay with sheepherder, mostly in silence, and share a big can of pork and beans with him. As quickly as we arrive, we take off to our unknown campground.

The evening light casts a million brilliant colors of reds and yellows as the sun goes down. The first twinkle of lights from Sand Draw can be seen as Samuel and I gather whatever wood we can find to start our bonfire.

As the flames leap up into the new fresh darkness, Samuel and I stand by the fire waving large back and forth waves, knowing Mom will be looking for the light of our bonfire and panning in the field glasses to focus on our smiling faces.

"'Gail Ann!" Dad calls out, "Come here."

I watch from the behind the screen door as my dad stands beside Mr. Meszkat in the hot June afternoon. I don't want to go near Mr. Meszkat.

Dad calls once again, and I open the screen door. I walk across the wood porch, dragging my feet with each step.

"Gail Ann, I told you to come here." His voice gets louder.

I cross the short distance over the dry, parched yard. A tumbleweed blows against my leg as I approach them. I lift my leg and rub the calf where the prickly weed brushed against me. I keep my eyes on the ground.

"What's wrong with you?" he scolds, waiting for no answer. "You go with Mr. Meszkat for some eggs."

Dad turns and walks toward the pickup idling in the driveway. The door slams, and a cloud of dust hides the pickup as it moves down the road. Dad does not look back.

Mr. Meszkat takes my hand; I am trying to pull it away. I smell tobacco juice. I don't like the smell of it.

"Please, Mr. Meszkat, let me go." I hear myself whisper.

Grandma Meszkat is away; I know what he will do.

The screen door opens; he scoops me up and carries me inside. I can't breathe; he has me tight.

His hands are big. He takes the back of my head with his right hand and twists hard so that my face is right before his. I close my eyes. I press my lips together and try to lock my jaw. No! I can smell him opening his mouth, then I feel his mouth on me. I clamp my jaw even tighter. He's trying to put his tongue in my mouth.

He forces my mouth open with his battering tongue.

I am crying. My eyes are wet; my face is wet. His great wet tobaccoy tongue is in my mouth. I am trying to breathe. I can't.

Mr. Meszkat is sitting down; he pulls me down with him and slams me between his legs. I am trying to get away.

I hear my voice saying "Pleeeeease, Mr. Meszkat, I promise I won't tell."

I hear his breathing. He takes his hand and puts it down into my jeans. He is running his finger down where I go to the bathroom.

I see the ashtray.

I am holding his wrist with both of my hands. He grabs my hair and pulls my head back. His whole hand is squeezing my crotch.

He takes his hand out of my jeans and opens his zipper on his pants and his peter, like Daddy has, is all big and straight. It smells funny like the mushroom cellar. I close my eyes. He is pulling my hair and holding my head back.

"Open your mouth," I hear him say in a funny voice.

The tears are running down my face.

"Please, Mr. Meszkat, let me go."

He takes my head and pushes it down so that my mouth goes over his thing as I am speaking. I can't breathe; it's like he's putting a whole hotdog in my mouth. I gag. I am going to throw up. His legs are wrapped around me; I can't move.

"Open your eyes, Gail Ann," he is saying as he jerks my head back.

I open my eyes, but I look at the ashtray. The sunlight coming through the window hits the ashtray—sparkling reds, blues, and greens.

Mr. Meszkat goes real stiff, and my face is all wet and sticky as he pees on me; but it's not yellow like when Peanuts or Daddy or Samuel pees. It's thick and white and sticky. He is peeing on me.

I watch his elbow hit the ashtray; and like a feather falling from my pillow, the ashtray falls to the floor.

He still has my hair in his hand. He is laughing and saying, "We can't send you home looking like that, can we, Gail Ann?"

"Let me go," I tell him.

He says, "As soon as we clean you up."

He stands up and zips his zipper. He grips me around the shoulders with his hands, pinning my arms to my body and carries me into the bathroom. He gets a lot of towels and then carries me back to the living room. My stomach hurts. I want to go home.

He sets me on a chair by the coat rack. He takes my shirt off. I am cold. He takes my hands and ties them together in front of me and pulls my arms up so that I am hanging from the coat rack.

He takes off my shoes and my jeans and then my underpants.

Just like Tom the turkey, I spin around and around.

He puts his hands all over me and says, "What a pretty little girl you are."

He goes away. I am crying without sound. I want Mom. I want to go home. I try to wiggle down from where I am hanging, but I only spin faster. It makes me dizzy.

He comes back into the room. In one hand, he has his open pocketknife; and in the other hand, he has a pail with water.

He sets the knife on the chair and the pail of water on the floor. From the pail of water, he takes a washrag and wrings it out. He wipes my face and whole body. The water feels warm.

He puts on my underpants, then my jeans, socks and shoes. Now he has the knife in his hand. I remember seeing the knife disappear in Tom's mouth and the blood gurgling down around Mr. Meszkat's hand onto the floor of the pen.

I watch his hand as he comes closer to me.

His face is right before my face, and he says, "It's our secret, isn't it, Gail Ann?"

And then he puts the blade of the knife on my lips.

CHAPTER 2

Home

The one-room schoolhouse sits a hundred feet or so off the main road of Sand Draw. It serves as a school, a town hall, a recreation center, and a home. It's a stone's throw away from the Roger's Cafe and Grocery Store where you can buy only milk and bread.

I can stand on the playground and look out and see my house far away in the distance. The playground, with a swing set, a small slide, and merry-go-round, is mostly small pebbles and barren patches of grass, eventually giving way to a vast prairie of sagebrush and cactus. It's in that prairie that Peanuts, when I ride him to school, grazes with his hobbled legs while I go to school.

It's a narrow, long building, with the classroom at the front door and Mr. and Mrs. Fullerton's living quarters in the back. A potbellied stove off to the right of the blackboard gives off an angry red glow in winter as it heats the classroom full of students.

This year, Mrs. Fullerton has students at every level from first to eighth grade. There are four of us in the second-grade class. We get to help with the first graders this year. The smallest class is the eighth graders; there are only two.

We stand at the rear of the schoolhouse at the entrance to the Fullerton's living quarters. It's suppertime, and we have been invited to share it with them.

Dad's balding head is very shiny. Mom has on the short-sleeved dress with big printed flowers that appear to dance as the billowing skirts make great circles around her when she turns. She smells of lilacs. Samuel and I are in jeans. I wear a white blouse; he has on a blue short-sleeved shirt.

Big brother Chris has opted to go to the Mason's.

The kids know Mr. Fullerton as Fred. We know Mrs. Fullerton as Mrs. Fullerton. Fred is a slight balding man with jaws like a hound dog. His expression is always the same—sad and mournful. He scurries around the school doing this and that and very rarely says a word.

"We have a special surprise," declares Mrs. Fullerton. "Fred has made a wonderful apple strudel."

Fred approaches the table showing a pan of a golden-looking rolled thing that smells great.

Samuel kicks me under the table. I turn and look and shrug my shoulders. He raises his eyebrows, puts his lips together tight, and shrugs his shoulders. We never thought that Fred could cook.

We watch as he cuts the strudel in generous proportions, pours thick cream over the top, and passes it down to each of us.

As I am about to take a bite, I drop my spoon. Samuel has a large spoonful approaching the huge cavern in his face. It disappears as he closes his mouth beginning to chew.

"Pfaaaaaaaaaa" comes a sound from Samuel as his mouth flies open and the apple strudel sprays across the table.

I drop my spoon again. I look over at Samuel; my head cocked to the side almost lying on my plate. I have one eye closed and my hand over my mouth trying to suppress a giggle.

"Why'd you do that?" I whisper with a laugh.

His tongue flutters as he takes the spoon and scrapes over it. Once again a series of "Pfaaaaaaaaaaa, pfaaaaaaaaaa" as he tries to spit all the strudel out.

My father is flushed a solid red.

Mom is in shock and has only looked with her mouth wide open.

Fred is frozen in horror.

Mrs. Fullerton has an arm in front of her face warding off flying particles of Fred's "wonderful" strudel.

"What the hell?" my father huffs as he rises from the table.

"It's salt," shouts Mrs. Fullerton as she takes a small taste of the great dessert. "It's salt!"

Saddling Peanuts is more luck than skill. He senses how short I am and when I struggle to place the saddle on his back and begin to tighten the cinch, I can see him take a deep breath and hold it. It makes his belly look like a barrel, and it's impossible to pull the cinch tight.

I try to wait until he has to let his breath out to take in fresh air, but he can really hold his breath long. Today, I have no patience.

As I stand on the stepladder, I place my knee against his belly and pull as tight as I can, hoping that it is sufficient. Straps pulled and tucked, I mount Peanuts and off I go. Mom had said that I could ride over to Sammy Gordon's house for the afternoon.

Coming up from the old creek bed, I can see the silver-colored pipes glistening in the early afternoon sun. Dad told me they call them "Christmas Trees." There is a big pipe in the middle with several small branches of pipes arranged up the sides. On each branch there are gauges and dials. This array of pipes is an automatic switching station for two or more gas lines that come together. When the process of switching takes place, most of us never know, but if you're nearby it makes a loud pinging sound.

As we approach the silver sculpture, Peanuts begins to perk up his ears and his nostrils flair. Maybe he has heard this pinging sound when he has been grazing the land and surely doesn't like it. I jerk the reins to the left to circle around.

Piiiiiing!

Peanuts jerks to the left just as I grab the saddle horn. The saddle twists to the right as the loose cinch belt no longer holds. The sagebrush is above my head. Falling.

A sharp pain and everything is dark.

I open my eyes, and the sky above is a dark blue, late evening blue. My head throbs, and I have the sense of being stiff.

Wait. Blank. I move my hand to my head and then I turn to lift myself up to a sitting position. Peanuts is a short distance away grazing. The saddle hangs beneath his belly. The reins from his halter drag slightly behind him as he moves forward tearing the grass off in neat little bunches.

A sharp pain rushes through my head as I stand. The Christmas tree is in the distance, silent.

Mom will be crazy with worry.

I walk gently toward Peanuts, wobbly and unsure. He continues to graze and easily goes with me as I grab the reins. I bring him to the gully, cinch the saddle belt, and sit myself in the saddle. Turning left, I make off toward home.

"Damn you, Ms. Annie," shouts Mom, and she comes running down the road from the house. "Damn you. You scared the shit out of me."

"I'm sorry," I cringe. "Peanuts got spooked, and I fell off." I put my hand to my head.

Mom grabs the halter on Peanuts and motions me to get down. She mumbles to herself, but I don't understand.

She lets loose of the halter as I jump to the ground. She turns me around then draws me roughly to her. She runs her fingers through my hair, half-caressing and half-searching for the bump.

Her hand stops, and she feels the bump on my head. "Oh my God, you could'a killed yourself." Big tears begin to roll from her eyes.

"Oh, Ms. Annie, I'd die, just die if anything happened to you."

It is snowing. I cannot see more than a few feet. The wind is blowing hard. I pull my scarf up around my mouth. It is cold. The snow is deep, over my knees. A big yellow lab dog, Moose, is right behind me her eyes closed against the swirling snow; large clumps of the powdery snow cling to her paws making it necessary to stop often to clean between her toes.

I turn around so the wind won't bite me. I hear the sound of a motor. Headlights from the Stockton's' old pickup loom before me as I walk backward.

"Gail Ann, that you?" shouts Mrs. Stockton through the open window of the pickup. "Get in here, before you freeze. I'll run you home."

I open the door. "Can Moose come too?" I don't wait for an answer as she jumps on the seat. It is warm inside the pickup.

The windshield wipers are going back and forth. The snow is like a brick wall. I can't see.

"How can you see, Mrs. Stockton?" I ask. The clattering sound of the snow chains hitting the fenders fills the cab. It's impossible to be heard.

We creep forward. I do not know where we are. I look at my watch. We have been driving for over an hour, and we are still not home.

We stop. "Are we lost, Mrs. Stockton?" I ask.

Mom is standing by the truck. I wonder how she got out here in the middle of nowhere. Then I see the outline of the house faintly in the short distance.

"God, Pauline I was so worried," she shouts above the wind. "Thanks for bringing her home. Come in, you can't leave here in this mess."

We both get out of the pickup. Moose bounds away into the white storm. I run to Mom and wrap my arms around her waist and bury my face in her scratchy wool coat.

Inside the house, I take off my coat. Mom turns around, and I see her eyes are red. Mrs. Stockton sees it too.

"Ruth, you okay?" she asks as she touches Mom's arm.

Mom turns away and then looks at me. Tears are rolling down her face. She bends down and wraps her arms around me. My face is ensconced in her breasts. "Oh, Pauline," she cries, "my mother just died about an hour ago."

Grandma lies on the bed; the white thin sheet falls on her profile like delicate lace. The coldness of the room comes through the crack of the door as I look, peeking in the dim light of the day. Snow occasionally swirls around the room as gusts of wind make their way through the open windows.

It's been snowing for three days, and we wait for the hearse to make the seventy-five-mile trip to take her body away. Dad had opened all the windows to prevent her from "smelling."

"Gail Ann," comes a faint voice, "please get away from that room." Mom gently puts one hand on my shoulder and with the other hand she reaches across and quietly closes the door.

Dad wiggles himself out the window as a rush of cold air fills the room. Standing on the windowsill, he grabs the edge of the roof and lifts himself up. The snow falls in great avalanches around his body.

As he reaches down, Mom hands him first the shovel, then the broom. The snow on the roof weighs heavy, and Dad begins to push the great piles from over the edge.

I count them one by one.

Bah-boom! Bah-boom!

I'm lying here beside Mom. While she sleeps, I press my ear ever closer to her breast, listening and counting the beats of her heart.

The rhythm that keeps my mother alive almost lulls me into sleep and then she stirs. I move my head away just as she turns her head toward me. She opens one eye and then the other. A smile spreads across her face.

"How come you're not sleeping?" She winks as she gives me a hug.

"I'm listening."

"To what?" She wrinkles her forehead as she releases me from the hug.

"You."

"Doing what?"

"Breathing"—I raise my eyebrows—"and your heart beating."

"You're so silly," she chides as she gathers me in her arms once again.

I put my ear once more against her breast and listen.

Bah-boom! Bah-boom!

CHAPTER 3

Moving On

The trip to town takes longer now. We have moved from Sand Draw to Crook's Gap. It's a company-owned town where we live in the bunkhouse and get our mail a half-hour drive away. Home on the Range. It's a bar, a general store, and the local post office.

The stars whiz by as I look through the car window. I turn my harmonica over and over in my hands. I am fighting sleep. Samuel is sitting up front with Mom, and he has already fallen asleep. The light from the dashboard gives an eerie glow to Mom's face as it is reflected in the front window glass. I am watching her eyes.

She brings the lighted cigarette to her mouth, takes a long slow drag, and then blows out the smoke through her mouth and nose. I scoot up toward the middle of the front seat and drape my arms over the top. I reach out and touch her upper arm.

"You tired, Gail Ann?" I see her eyes look in the rearview mirror, and she smiles at me.

"Ya," I hear myself whine. "How much longer before we're home?"

"Oh, another twenty-five or thirty miles." She smiles at me in the rearview mirror. "Why don't you lie down and sleep, sweetheart?"

I throw myself against the backseat and sigh. I like going to town, but I hate the long ride back. I wish we didn't live so far away. The swaying of the car and the dull roar of the motor are fading in the background.

I'll close my eyes. Dark. Floating. Light.

Bang! I am thrown against the floor. Confusion. Where am I? Squealing tires. Rubber burning. Back and forth. Voices. A scream. No movement. Silence. Cramped, pain.

"Gail Ann! Samuel! Oh, Jesus, are you kids all right?"

I turn my head. I am looking up. Mom is bending over the backseat looking down at me. She grabs my arm and pulls me up to the seat. I see Samuel who is looking at me. I begin to cry.

"Mom, what happened?" I ask, "Did we have a wreck?"

She shakes her head no and wipes my tears.

"There is something in the road. I swerved to miss it." She gets out of the car. "Must be an antelope or deer. I'm sorry, kids."

She reaches under the seat for the flashlight. She walks back to the spot where she thinks the thing in the road might be. Samuel and I are looking at the spot of light as it makes its way down the road.

The spot stops; there in the light is not a deer or antelope but a man.

She is calling to us. We run to her. There on the road, the man is lying face up, twisted unnaturally. He is moaning. Mom bends down. I am terrified. Samuel takes my hand. Mom stands up.

"I can't move him," she says almost to herself. "I think his back is broken."

She takes the flashlight and beams it around the road and off toward the barrow pit. There on its top with a door torn off and the roof caved in is his pickup. She motions for Samuel and me to follow, and she goes over to the truck.

"I need a board or something straight," she says, but there is nothing.

We walk back toward the car. Mom opens the trunk and gets out an old blanket and another flashlight. We walk back to the man on the road, and she puts the blanket on him.

"Samuel and Gail Ann listen to me and listen good." She brushes her hair back from her forehead. "The man is hurt, real bad. If I move him, I might hurt him more, or worse, he might die."

She pauses.

"If we go and get help, he might get hit like we almost hit him," she kneels down beside us. She takes us in her arms. "You have to help me . . . Oh, God, believe me, Mom doesn't want to do this, but I have to go get help and you two have to watch and see that he doesn't get run over. Do you understand me?"

"Mom, I can do it alone," Samuel says softly, "Gail Ann doesn't have to stay."

"I wanna help too," I say.

Mom explains to us that it is easier with two of us watching. Sweetwater Gas Station is just up fifteen miles, and she will be right back with help. We are to take the flashlights and wave them if we see headlights coming up the road. She explains to us to stay off the road, even if a car is coming.

"Don't get into any cars till I get back, ya hear me!" she says as she gets in the car. She is starting the motor. She drives away; the taillights fading in the distance as she picks up speed.

The glow of the prairie gets brighter as our eyes become used to the dark. We are standing on the edge of the barrow pit, back to back. Samuel watches one way; I watch the other. The man is still, but we can hear him breathing.

"I'm scared," I whisper to Samuel.

"Me too," he whispers back.

The glow of the prairie is fading, up the road comes a pair of headlights. Samuel and I wave frantically to warn the oncoming car. It slows and then stops. The headlights glare in our faces; we both hear the door open. It's Mom; she came back. I feel the smile spread across my face.

"They're coming kids. Soon." She takes us both in her arms and kisses the tops of our heads.

"I mean, I mean, Jolene. I mean it's time to . . . I mean . . . go home," says Mr. "I Mean" Welch.

I have a hard time understanding Jolene's Dad because of all his "I mean". His tongue is thick, and Jolene and I both know that her dad has had too much to drink. She looks at me and rolls her eyes back into her head.

Tonight I am staying with Jolene. Dad told me to stay with them because he wasn't going back home. He had other business. He thinks I don't know that he's going with Mrs. Murphy. She owns a ranch down at Split Rock. He goes with Mrs. Murphy when Mom is sick in the hospital. I want to go visit Mom, but it's too far.

Jolene's mom and dad are sitting at the bar. The music is blasting on a jukebox in the back of the room. Over the bottles in the back of the counter, up above the mirror is a set of antelope antlers framing the sign: Home on the Range, Wyoming. I hate this bar. It's always smoky, and everybody smells of beer.

"Jesus, I mean Jesus . . . look at them dogs. I mean, that ole boy is really, I mean, pumpin'," shouts I Mean Welch.

Outside the big picture window, Jolene's hound is humping Beulah Johnson's ole yellow dog. Jolene and I run to the window. Several of the men are laughing and shouting in the background.

"You know what they're doing?" Jolene asks me.

"Sure, makin' puppies." Jolene knows that too. She is testing me. I don't like to watch. I turn and walk away. Nowhere to go, just wait.

I look at the clock, it is 1:30 in the morning and we are still here. Jolene's mom is sitting in the pickup, snoring. I Mean is drinking another beer. He gets up and weaves and sways toward the door.

Outside in the parking lot, he drops the keys. I hear Jolene pleading with her dad, "Please, Pap, don't drive. It's okay. We'll get home."

Her dad says something, but I don't understand. He gets in the back of the pickup. He lies down and doesn't move. Jolene's dog jumps up beside him.

"Gail Ann, we gotta get home. Can you drive?" asks Jolene.

"No, but I can shift gears. Mom's been teaching me on the Jeep."

We jump into the pickup. I sit in the middle. Jolene is behind the wheel. She starts up the motor. I turn on the lights.

Jolene and I are driving down the road. She tells me when to shift, and we both keep our eyes on the road.

I am crying. I toss another stone in the creek. I wonder if humans have babies the same way as animals. I heard Dean Stockton, Dad's work buddy, say that Mrs. Murphy had twins.

"Ole Shorty Westbrook's bastard kids," he said.

I wonder where that puts Mom. I don't think I was supposed to hear them talking about it. He said she delivered them alone. What did he mean?

"Well, at least they were boys," Dean said.

I hate Dad sometimes.

School District 25 is a prairie school district. It has this responsibility to manage kids isolated by vast distances to attend school once they reach a certain level. My two brothers are now entering junior high school. Mom and Dad have decided that maintaining two separate households is best. Boarding out the two boys to other families was not the answer. I'll go to Ash Grove Elementary School in Riverton where there are more students in my classroom than we had in our whole school.

Our house is on the corner of a busy street, and it sounds
like thunder when the cars roll over the culvert where the
water from the irrigation ditch runs through.

The cat howls.

"Don't, please, Chris! Don't throw her in the water," I am
screaming.

"Ah, Gail Ann, it's just a damn ole stray cat. Besides cats
have nine lives."

He laughs, then Chris raises the cat just above his head
and with one heave, throws it into the swirling water. My
stomach churns.

The muddy water gulps the cat like a frog takes an insect.
Just below where the cat went into the water, she fights her way
to the top. The wild look in her eyes; a window to fear.

She frantically paddles toward the edge of the ditch,
crying in terror, waiting for the horror she has known before.
I am with her in each stroke she takes, helping her fight the
current.

Chris is shouting with glee as the cat approaches the culvert
where the funnel of water disappears to the black depths of
the pipe.

"In the arms of God, there is peace!" his words resting
heavily on peace. Mom sits beside me, her eyes filled with
tears, and her bottom lip is quivering. She grips tightly the
small song book.

"Let Jesus Christ fill your heart. Let him share your
burdens and make the load lighter." His words rise and fall.
A strong emphasis on Jesus Christ.

Each time he calls out "Come forward and take Jesus
Christ as your savior," I see someone step out and with bowed
head proceed to the altar where he quietly says "Bless you,
lamb of God."

"I CAN F-E-E-E-L THE POWER OF GOD CALLING HIS
LOST LAMBS!" he brings his hands in an upward scooping
motion.

Mom reaches out her hand and takes mine, pulling me toward the aisle. I jerk away from her and violently shake my head.

She leans toward me and quietly whispers in my ear. "Please, Ms. Annie"—she takes my hand once again—"I can't go alone, and Mom really needs this."

Mom always calls me Ms. Annie when she is mad at me or when she needs something.

We move out toward the aisle. Mom walks forward with her head bowed. I walk slightly behind her and watch the altar loom before us.

My cheek burns like fire where Mom has struck me. I glare at her. I fight the tears that hang on the edge of my eyes. I won't damn it. I won't give her the satisfaction of letting her know she got to me.

"The Bible says to turn the other cheek," I hiss.

"Go right ahead." She look me straight in the eye with one eyebrow slightly raised. "See if it makes a difference."

I turn my head exposing the other cheek. With the broad part of her hand, she slaps me once more. I reel back with the sting of it. I look at her in disbelief. I begin to cry, tears streaming down my face.

"Bitch!" I say through clinched teeth.

"Wouldn't bother me to do it again!" she cautions. She turns to leave my room and then stops before exiting.

"When you're ready to talk rationally," she glances back at me, "I'll be in the living room." She exits. I throw the pillow at the door.

I open my eyes from a deep sleep. Completely alert as if in the continuation of a dream I lie here not moving, listening. There. It is the sound that did it—soft, muffled, barely audible. It can't be Mom; she's in the hospital.

I throw back the covers and quietly sit on the edge of the bed. Carefully I lift myself off the bed. Slowly, slowly. I take the first step. I am biting my tongue as if that might help to prevent making a noise. One step after the other, toe then roll to heel, inch after inch. I put my hand on the doorknob and twist ever so slightly. Grasping the handle hard and then harder. Pulling the door with patience, I look through the crack.

From my bedroom, I can see that the back door is open. The screen door is pulled to. Dad's profile is silhouetted against the moonlit sky. He doesn't see me. I try to figure out what he's watching. I turn my head every so slightly; I can see through the kitchen window. There is a light at the next-door neighbor's upstairs. I look at Dad once again. Movement. I glance once more at the window. It's Louise, one of my classmates. The son-of-a-bitch is watching Louise.

I can't believe I am standing here looking at this concert of action and reaction. She's undressing, and he's watching her.

I watch him reach for the zipper of his pants. He pulls out his swollen penis.

I clasp my hand tightly over my mouth as I gag. I stand here watching my old man jerk off.

Closing the door, I turn and return to the bed. I sit; and with clenched fists, I hit and hit the fleshy parts of my upper thighs.

CHAPTER 4

Nebraska

We often went to Nebraska to visit my Aunt Jean and Uncle Ralph. The year I turned thirteen was no different, only this time I stayed—for two years.

I hear a car come up the driveway. The gravel crunches under the tires. It must be Uncle Ralph. I get up from the dining room table and look out the kitchen window. The taillights of the old blue Plymouth go into the garage.

The yard light goes on, and Uncle Ralph, with the bill of his cap cocked to one side, weaves across the short span to the front door. Lassie, his dog, greets him with a wag of his tail. The screen door to the porch squeaks and then the storm door into the house opens wide.

I am at the sink, running cold water into a glass. As Uncle Ralph comes in the kitchen, the smell of beer and peanuts fill my nostrils. The cigar, long since burnt out, is still set at the corner of his mouth. His eyes are glazed, and he's having problems focusing.

"Hello, Gail Ann," he says with a thick tongue.

I nod in recognition as I am drinking the fresh cold water. He turns left into the dining room; I follow him. I still have some Algebra problems to finish up. I sit down at the table. He goes to the archway into the living room, flips on the television, sits down, and quietly watches.

I look at the clock. It's been an hour since Uncle Ralph came home and he hasn't said anything. I put my paper together, slide the chair under the table, and start to walk to the stairwell leading to my bedroom upstairs.

He is behind me. He reaches out and touches my arm. I freeze.

"Gail Ann," he whispers softly.

I whirl around and look directly into his eyes. I don't want to show him that I am afraid. "Don't!" I hiss and then back off. "You startled me, please don't touch me."

He drops his hand, and his eyes look to the floor.

"Gail Ann, Jean is not here. Will you sleep with me!"

I want to scream, and I want to yell, What the hell is it that they use me. Oh, Jesus, no . . . not again.

"I don't want to do anything and . . . and you don't have to do anything. I just want to sleep with you. It's been . . ." he continues in a boyish pleading voice.

"No! Damn it, Uncle Ralph, you've been drinking," I glare at him. "Oh, Jesus, listen to what you are saying. You're gonna feel rotten in the morning."

I open the door to the stairwell and run upstairs. I enter my bedroom and slam the door shut. I lock it. I throw myself on the bed, crying.

Aunt Jean is angry with me. The accident with the tractor will cost over $400. I knocked the corncrib completely off the foundation. I didn't mean to. I was too anxious to please. I had learned how to drive the tractor and I just wanted to park it where it belonged. Putting the gearshift in road gear made it jump forward at the slightest touch of the accelerator.

She reminds me that Mom and Dad have sent me here so that I could learn responsibility; to give Mom a break.

"It's not true," I shout. "I wanted to stay."

She slaps me across the face. I put my hand on my cheek.

"You will be the death of your mother!" she growls.

The awards banquet is held in the church recreation room. Everyone is here. I am excited. Tonight I will get my award. Aunt Jean will finally see that I can do things right. The names are being called one by one. Each of the young girls walks forward and gets their letter.

"For excellence in volleyball. Gail Westbrook, First-Year Letter."

I take the letter from Coach Rhoan. I am looking for Aunt Jean. I want her to know that about my award. I do not see her.

As I walk back to my seat, my friend Donna grabs my hand and says, "Good for you, Gail."

I see Aunt Jean through the church window. She is carrying a garbage can. She wasn't in the recreation room; she was helping to clean up the kitchen.

CHAPTER 5

College

It was time to go back, to return to my family and in my junior year of high school I was home again—a new house, a different town, but home. Graduation from high school saw me off to nursing school.

We represent an entire spectrum of ages and experiences. We all made our way down to Arapahoe Street in Denver to attend our first class in chemistry with the University of Colorado Denver extension.

The professor is a tall lanky man, slightly bald, with a beautiful baritone voice. Someone told me he was over 75, had a wife that was in her twenties and a young son of about two. Well he certainly knew about chemistry.

He introduces himself, slowly looks out over our class and then quietly states, "My patience shall last as long as your uncertainty."

He has captured us all and put us at ease. I am going to like this class.

He then begins the role call of names. "Miss Kathy Ankor," pauses and waits for the ubiquitous "here." On down the line he goes, calling out the first name and last name, rather uneventful, but we all politely listen.

"Ms Roberta La Pea," he calls out. No answer, everyone looks around for a Roberta La Pea. We have no Roberta La Pea in our class.

Realization spreads across our faces like water spilling over the edge of a glass filled too full. A young, dark haired man slowly rises and says, "Sir, my name is Mister Robert LePe. It's French."

"Welcome," the professor continues, not missing a beat.

Robert will forever be Roberta La Pea.

Jani is an x-ray technician student; we have become fast friends. I am often here at her house, studying or just hanging out. Her boy friend Joe is not a family favorite, but it doesn't matter her Mom is mostly absent and Jani continues her involvement with him. Her mom always likes it when I am here. She feels Jani is studying rather than playing.

"You want some more lasagna?" asks Jani.

I shake me head. "God no, I'm goina bust if I take another bite." I pat my stomach. "I have to study chem."

Jani stands up, comes to me, and touches my arm. *Electric.* I know she wants me to cover for her if her mom calls. Joe is coming over.

The telephone rings and I answer it. Jani's mom is on the phone and wants to speak with Jani. I lie and tell her that Jani has run to get some soda; I will have her call when she gets back.

"Hey, Jani," I call as I open the door to her bedroom. I stop. There on the bed lies Jani, and Joe is on top of her fuckin' away.

Oh, shit! No! I turn and run out of the room. How could she?

The room in the dorm is dark. I throw on the light switch. Empty beer cans are scattered everywhere. My classmates are there. Kathy lies on her back on the bottom bunk. Jani haphazardly draped over a chair, her head lying on the desk; on the top bunk snoring loudly is Susan. Nobody gets drunk on 3.2 beer! On the floor I see an empty pint of peppermint schnapps.

The bathroom door is slightly cracked. I open it farther, the smell of vomit. Jesus! If Guay decides to do a Saturday night dorm check, we have had it.

I want to take Jani back to the x-ray students' wing but first got to get these beer cans out of here. One by one I place them in the paper bag. Sit the bag on the floor. I go in the bathroom and clean the vomit off the toilet bowl. I spray air freshener in a heavy dose. Shit! I know I shouldn't have bought the beer for them.

11:45 PM. Curfew is in fifteen minutes. I pick up the bag of trash, scurrying down the hallway. My eyes are darting back and forth, constantly searching for someone, anyone. I turn the corner toward the long passage to the front door. Not locked yet.

"Oomph!" R-i-i-i-p. Crash! Clang! Clang! Clang! Clang! The beer cans roll and clatter to an earsplitting silence. Before me is Guay, the Great White Angel; and she is sitting on the floor.

"Ms. Westbrook, do you understand the gravity of your offense?"

I nod.

"Please rise."

I stand, lifting a hundred pounds of bricks it seems.

Guay, the Great White Angel, the Director of the School of Nursing quietly passes judgment on my actions. I'm going home. I have violated a school policy, possession and consumption of alcohol on campus grounds.

I open the door to our dorm room. Susan, Jani, and Kathy are patiently waiting for me. They say nothing, but the questions are in their eyes.

"They know nothing about you three—keep your mouths shut."

They hug me.

I look around the bus and pick an empty seat. Brushing the crumbs off the cushion, I sit down. The nurse everyone expects me to be won't be coming home in starchy whites after all.

The bus screeches to a halt. Supper break. It's snowing out. Hell, I only lasted for four months.

"Folks be back on the bus in thirty minutes," announces the bus driver.

I make my way to the counter and sit on the stool. Should go to the bathroom first. Everyone will probably do that. I twirl around on the rotating stool; across the way sits a young woman looks a lot like Jani.

"Hey you! Girl! Ya goina order or just sit there?"

I spin around.

"Oh . . . ah sorry. Tuna sandwich and a glass of milk."

The sandwich arrives on mushy white bread. I should complain, for what? I take a few bites and drop the tasteless food back on the plate. At least the milk is good.

Tossing the money on the counter, I make my way to the public toilet.

"Greyhound to Cheyenne, Laramie, and Rawlins. Departing at door 5," crackles the loud speaker.

The big snowflakes hit the window as we creep out on the highway. It is hard to see. I lay my head on the back of the seat close my eyes for a moment. My leg starts to cramp. I stand up in the aisle. Almost everyone is asleep. The trip will be longer today if it keeps snowing like this. Doesn't matter, I'm not sure how well I am going to face Mom. Toward the back of the bus is the young blond woman that reminded me of Jani. She is kissing some guy next to her. I try to look away.

I shake my head. The blonde and her kissing buddy are staring at me. I drop my eyes. Turn and slump down in the seat. The bus is slowing down.

"Rawlins," he calls out.

I look out the window. A tall auburn-haired woman is standing underneath the street lamp. Snow is whirling around her. I grab my bag and make my way toward the door of the bus. I take a deep breath and step down off the bus.

I look up. "Hi, Mom."

"Hi," she says. She puts her arm around my shoulder. "Welcome home."

CHAPTER 6

Enlistment

I always wanted to go in the military, my leaving nursing school just changed the date I would be going.

The miles melt as the bus speeds along the highway toward Denver. Enlistment day—provided I've lost all the weight I needed. The scales this morning reminded me that I was right at the borderline. If I eat another salad, I'll turn into a rabbit. I'd kill for a banana split. My stomach does a flip-flop. Tomorrow at this time I'll be in Alabama. Sounds funky, unromantic, who in the hell goes to Alabama? The only thing I know about Alabama is that it's known as the "Heart of Dixieland" (Is that music or a place?).

The bus pulls into the main station in downtown Denver. I grab my bag and walk to the taxi stand.

"Old Custom House on Sixteenth and Arapaho," I say as I get into the cab.

Shit! Still three pounds overweight. I back down off the scale. Sergeant Bingham leaves the room. I head back toward the wall and lean against it. Waiting.

Sergeant Bingham walks in. "Gail, you ever been in a sauna?"

I shake my head. She grabs my arm and pulls me toward the exit. Half-walking, half-running, she drags me across the street. A big sign above our heads—Sixteenth Street Gym—

quickly disappears as we enter the door. Before I have time to protest, Sergeant Bingham throws a bath towel at me.

"Strip and wrap this around you." She turns and walks away.

Without resistance, I undress and put the towel around me. Just as I am wondering what to do next, a short stocky woman comes in and motions for me to follow her. We walk into a room filled with what looks like bathtubs and other strange gadgets. In the corner is a white cabinet like machine that looks like a washer. I saw a picture of one in the Sears catalog. She opens the cabinet, and it reminds me of a stool sitting between two gigantic jaws.

Two hours have gone by with those jaws wrapped around me. The steam is "chewing" away at those extra pounds. The stocky woman comes in the room followed by Sergeant Bingham.

"You go to the right," she points. "She'll need some help," she motions to Sergeant Bingham.

The woman opens the jaws, and the cool air rushes in like cold water and sends a chill through me. I try to stand up, but it seems I am glued to the stool. They grab my arms. My legs feel like rubber. They assist me over to the scale. Five-and-a-half pounds melted away.

In the middle of the night, after having traveled what seemed like a million miles, I am weighed, measured, and escorted to a huge room filled with beds wrapped in khaki blankets. The beds are lined up perfectly straight, heel to toe. Occasionally a bed is occupied by some woman. A fan roars at the end of a long empty aisle; it glistens in the evening light. It is here I wait until my basic training platoon is filled.

She walks up to me, and I look up. I have never seen such a tall woman. She looks me straight in the eye.

"Ya'll have any cohens?" she drawls.

I hesitate. My mind is clicking and sorting. I shrug my shoulders and turn to her.

"I'm sorry, I don't know what a cohen is."

"Ya'll know what I mean, quarters, d-i-imes, and nickels," she smiles.

"Oh! You mean coins."

"That's what I said cohens."

I am waiting for my audition. I keep thinking this is a mistake. How in the hell did they know I played a trombone?

Two sergeants are having an argument—not the first time.

"Okay . . . damn it Eleanor . . . the next son-of-a-bitch who can blow the Goddamn thing has got it."

I enter a large room. The instruments of the band lie still upon polished brass stands. The one sergeant who was arguing steps toward me and hands me a trombone.

"Blow!" she bellows.

I put the mouthpiece to my lips and somehow manage to blow the best tone I've ever made.

She steps forward, takes the trombone, and says, "Personnel will notify you if you passed the audition."

(Don't call us, we'll call you.) "Yes, Sergeant," I sputter as I walk out of the room.

The light filters through the window at the front of the chapel. We march in methodically, take our place, and wait for the cue to sit. I stare at the image on the window. Pallas Athena the goddess of war and peace. "Colonel Bogey March" softly played by a small group from the band echoes throughout the chapel. Arched over the window in bold black letters: **WISDOM, ACHIEVEMENT, CHARACTER.** Basic training is over, and now we will all receive a piece of paper that tells us that we have crossed the first barrier.

The music has stopped playing. First Sergeant asks all guests to rise; I see the chaplain walk up to the mike.

"Let us pray," he says. There is a slight movement as heads are automatically bowed. I glance at the first sergeant. Her eyes meet mine. Our heads are not lowered. I drop my eyes.

"Amen." The cue is given to sit down. Captain Biltworth rises and walks to the speaker's stand and begins introducing the WAC Center director. Lieutenant Colonel Larceners takes her elegant self and stands before us.

"You have begun your date with destiny," she begins.

CHAPTER 7

Assignments

Everyone is in place. The women in crisp green summer uniforms fill each row. Highly polished shoes glisten under the lights in the room. I am in an alien section, back with the drums. I am to be the foundation from which all music will be played.

Earlier in the month I remember the left . . . left . . . left, right, left. One hundred twenty beats to a minute. Thirty-inch steps. We marched back and forth from the PX to the band building. Everywhere I walk the rhythm haunting all my thoughts. This is my big chance. Sgt. Lewis, the bandleader, informed me that I would be given a chance. "Special privilege," she said. I knew in my heart it was because of my upper body strength. I could easily carry the bass drum during those long parades.

I look toward the front of the room. My usual seat—last chair in third trombone—is painfully vacant. Sergeant Somerville once again without full section. Seven months I have struggled to make it with the trombone section. Sergeant Somerville finally confessed and said I had a great tone quality. That was sort of a backhanded compliment.

All around everyone is playing scales and warming up their instruments. The senior clarinetist sounds the tuning note on her clarinet. All other sections adjust as needed. I have long ago tightened the heads and polished and pampered my instrument.

The palm of my hand itches. I scratch it and realize that it is damp. Nerves? Yes! Scooter tosses me a small white hand towel.

"Psssst!" I look around. It's Gwen, letting go of her French horn. She winks and gives me a thumbs up. Claire, her piccolo close to her lips, gives me the okay sign.

Tap, tap, tap. A signal is given from the conductor's stand. There is absolute quiet.

"Okay! Page 5, 'Washington Post March.' The conductor looks straight at me. Ruffling of paper breaks the silence.

She raises her baton. The rhythm begins to tick in my head. When the baton makes a full circle and hits the imaginary bottom, I know I must hit the bass drum with my mallet.

Her hands sweep up. Time and all energy are frozen in that one movement. All sound begins as I hit the drum. It's working. At each chop of her baton I hear the deep sound of my instrument signaling to all around the rhythm is set.

Someone says something. What? I take my eyes away from her hands. Oops, go back. Sounds funny. More voices. Frantically scanning the sheet of music. Where is the beat? I look in panic at Sergeant Lewis. She is saying something. I don't understand. Failure . . . you screwed up, Westbrook. This was a mistake. Heat rises in my face. I got to get out of here. The mallet becomes my frustration. I no longer hit the drum. I cock the mallet behind my head and look straight at the open window. I toss it like a knife. In slow motion with perfect aim, it goes out the window. I am walking. I see the door. Got to get out. Got to run.

"You want another beer? Gwen asks.

"No," I shake my head. "I really don't like the taste of beer."

God! I have to pee! But I just can't, not now. If I pee, I'll chicken out.

Silence.

"Gwen"—I lick the corner of my mouth—"can I ask you something?"

Dumb, dumb, Gail, of course you can ask her something. It's darker than the inside of a cow out here. Jesus, I wonder how we would explain what two women were doing in the middle of nowhere parked in a car drinking beer?

"Sure," she quietly answers.

I turn on the key and the dashboard lights cast a faint glow. I reach for the knob to turn on the radio hoping to find some mood music. Between crackles and pops I find "The Stripper."

"Nervous?" she asks. I don't dare answer that question.

"What would you say if I told you I like you," I spit out.

"That's nice," she teases. Was that a chuckle I heard?

"I mean . . . Oh shit! This is hard." I blow out a mouthful of air.

"What?" she looks at me with a scowl.

I brush my hand through my hair. "I mean like more than friends?"

"I would say 'What are you doing over there'?" She moves and sits with her back against the door.

Oh my god! Now what do I do? An exquisite pain shoots through me. I freeze. I'm sitting here panting like a damn dog. I clench and unclench my hands.

She takes my closed fist in her hand and gently pulls me toward her. My arms encircle her, and I smell her freshly washed hair as she snuggles to my shoulder.

I am thirteen again. Myrna is my pretend date in this silly little game we play. It's a game for them, but not for me. Carol is mad because she got Jonnie—and nobody likes Jonnie as a date 'cause she has chapped lips.

I take my fingers and run them across Gwen's lips—soft, soft as hell. I turn her face and skim her lips with mine. I kiss her hard, realizing my insistence as we kiss.

She takes my hand and leads it to the soft mound of flesh—her breast, the nipple, hard, pushes against the palm of my hand as I cover it. Oh God! I really think I'm goina die.

"Hey, Westbrook, you gotta button open!" someone says to me as she passes by.

"Huh?" I do a double take and then quickly look down at my uniform jacket searching for an open button. My head is not screwed on right this morning.

"Touch me," she whispers.

I look around swearing I heard someone say something. It must be written all over my face. I feel like a neon light blinking in absolute darkness. I am afraid to look at her this morning. My puppy dog look will certainly give me away.

We drive up to the barracks. I turn off the motor, and we sit in silence. She puts her hand on the door handle.

"Don't go," I hesitate as I turn to look at her. "Not yet"

"We can't stay out here," she says. "It might look suspicious."

"How come it got suspicious all of a sudden?" I puzzle, draping my arms over the steering wheel, locking fingers. "We've sat out in the car before. A helluva lot longer than we have now."

"That was before tonight."

"I just touched you," I whisper. "We didn't carve anything in stone."

"Silly." She reaches out and touches my arms and quickly withdraws. "It's different. Trust me, it's different."

"Are you saying I am going to regret this?"

"You might."

I shake my head. "I don't think so."

Here she comes! My heart pounds against my chest. I just want to scream out loud. Oh God Gwen! I don't regret anything. It was wonderful! I cast my eyes downward. I walk quickly toward my instrument case and pull the shiny trombone from its cradle. Dummy! Why didn't you speak to her?

"Hi, Gail." She looks at me with a slight wrinkle in her forehead.

"Hi," I say with my mouth half-closed hoping my heart won't leap out. I practically run toward my seat. I glance at her quickly as she pulls the French horn from its place and walks toward her section.

The two tones of her breast are magnificent. I take her nipple between my lips.

"Westbrook!" comes the commanding voice.

My eyes dart everywhere. I look up and see Sergeant Somerville standing before me. She is smiling. Does she know?

"You could blow that trombone better if you used a mouthpiece," she chides.

My earlobes begin to burn as I realize that I have my trombone to my lips without the mouthpiece.

"Claire, have you seen Gwen?"
She shakes her head.
"Thanks."

"Goddamn it, Gail. You're closing in too fast!"

"What the hell? You were the one—" I turn to go.

Gwen reaches and touches my arm. I spin around and throw her hand off.

"Shit! You're just like Scooter!" she shouts through clinched teeth.

"Scooter? What has Scooter got to do with this?"

"You're so damn ignorant . . . so Goddamn ignorant!" she hisses.

I walk through the building. Searching each latrine and the laundry room. I have walked outside in the grassy area by the creek, and she is nowhere in sight. I look back toward the building, searching each window on the three floors of the barracks hoping to see her leaning out. I kick a stone, put my hands in my pocket and walk back toward the entrance.

"Hey, Westbrook!" It's long, tall, lanky Scooter. Her beady eyes are checking me out.

"Hi, Sergeant Smith." I can't call her Scooter except when Gwen and I talk. I quickly keep walking. I head for the full band room. I want to pick up some music to look over. I'll just have to wait until Gwen makes up her own mind to come back when she wants to and then she may not want to talk to me.

I hesitate. I hear a slight noise. I scan the room with my eyes. Going over to the wall, I throw on the overhead lights. Nothing. I turn off the light except the one by the door. I walk over to the instrument cage. The tuba horn case is open and lying there curled up is Gwen. She is full in sleep.

"Gwen," I whisper. Her eyes slowly open. She looks around. Her eyes return to my face, and she smiles. I sit down on the floor by the tuba case. She rolls on her side to face me, her hand cradling her cheek.

"Hi," she whispers.

"Gwen, what did you mean about Scooter?"

"Gail, Gail, Gail. I had to start somewhere too!"

"Scooter? Really? Do you still . . . a . . . a care for her? Jesus!

"Come on. Let's get out of here." Gwen jumps up and closes the case. Carefully avoiding touching me, she motions for me to follow her. As I jump up from the floor, I reach and flip off the switch.

We sit in the hotel room. Mom is sleeping. She traveled all the way to Kansas City just to see the band concert. She shouldn't have. I hope she doesn't wake up. I just can't seem to get these tears to stop. Her kidney disease is slowly eating away at her.

As I look up from my comic book, Mom hesitates as she walks toward the counter to pay for the milk. She grabs a hold of a corner on the display case. The room is empty. She whispers to me in desperation, "Gail Ann, hurry, come here." She melts to the floor. Her eyes roll back in her head. A dark stain creeps through her dress, flows slowly over the floor. Her legs and shoes covered in the black/red color of her blood.

Her breathing is heavy. I look how tight the skin is stretched on her body. The fluid buildup makes her seem so large. She stirs. I reach out and touch her. She opens her eyes. Smiles. Those perfect white teeth peek out from behind well-defined lips.

"I was dreaming," she says, "you got married."

I sigh.

I kiss Gwen full on the mouth. It's like biting down on a hot marshmallow.

'You never say anything about Don."

"He's dead, Mom. What is there to say?"

She shrugs her shoulders and winces in pain.

"You weren't going to marry him anyhow, would you?" she says matter-of-factly. "You won't marry anybody."

We returned from the Kansas City tour. Gwen and I have decided to take a ride. Time to steel a moment or two.

Her head lies softly against the back of the seat. The glow from the car radio casts shadows against the dark circles of her breast. Her blouse lies entirely open. Her breathing slowly returns to long measured intakes. I kiss her neck and then begin to move toward the slight rise of her breast. My hand still remains with her, tightly held, surrounded in the warm moist fluid generated by the urgency of our lovemaking.

She bolts straight up. "Headlights!" she cries with panic. I jerk my head up. She lifts her body from my hand. Her face winces in slight pain. I move behind the steering wheel. Gwen, with swift movements, fastens her blouse. She grabs her clothes and bolts out the door of the car.

The MP car pulls directly in front of mine. Opening the door, the MP walks toward me, swinging the flashlight in large sweeps.

"What you doing way out here?" he asks as his eyes search inside the car.

"She brought me out here so I could pee," shouts Gwen from the rear of the car. The MP, startled, turns quickly toward the rear and shines his flashlight in the direction of her voice. Gwen is squatting at the rear of the car. He quickly turns the flashlight away.

I shrug my shoulders. "She had to pee."

He clears his throat and begins to walk away. "Well, don't stay out here, it's no place for girls to be alone."

He opens the door to the MP car and starts up his motor. He spins in a tight circle and drives away.

As the red glow of the taillights fade, Gwen enters the car, flopping down in the seat. She throws her head against the seat. I start up the car.

"Jesus! That was close," she says breathlessly, "No more!" I look at her.

She touches my arm and looks straight at me, "At least in the car."

Gwen puts her fingers to her lips and points in the direction of the laundry room. Without question, I walk directly to the door and push it open. I turn and begin to speak, "What the hell!"

Again she puts her finger to her lips and shakes her head. Pulling on my arm she walks through to the clothes dryers.

She turns the knobs and pushes the dial. The machine begins its loud rhythmic tumbling action.

"They pulled one of the women in for questioning," she whispers.

"Who?" I ask.

"CID." She drops her voice.

"Shit!" I clinch my hand into a fist. "When?"

"Yesterday! Bear says they got the whole place bugged."

"Bull! How does she know?" I glance around thankful that the dryer is so loud. "She ever fined one?"

The sun is coming up over the trees. Gwen and I are leaning out of the barracks window. Where is our best buddy Claire? We have played two-handed poker for the last four hours. Claire had told us that she would bring the car back by one.

The salesman is a typical stereotype of the fly-by-night car dealer. Our multi-owner, candy apple red Jeep, complete with musical notes painted over all and an oogah horn capped with a trombone mute has breathed its last. We all stand around, pat it with love, and fondly remember it was that type of vehicle that when you go to the filling station you say "fill it up with oil and check the gas." Before us, our new—very used 1951 Oldsmobile complete with air conditioner that doesn't work. Each of us in turn gives the man our share of the money. We are excited.

"We should've gone with her," mutters Gwen.

"I hate the NCO Club," I say matter-of-factly.

Last night was Claire's turn to use the car. She always went to the NCO Club. The club closed at one, so we expected her shortly after. When she didn't show up by two, we figure she must have met some guy and went for a bite to eat. Wimpy Burger stayed open till three.

"Hey look! Here she comes," cries Gwen. She grabs my arm and drags me behind her as we take the stair two at a time down to the front door.

We run outside and down the street where Claire has parked the car. She hasn't got out of the car. As we approach, we can see Claire has her arms draped over the steering wheel, her head is bent down in her arms.

Gwen opens the door. "Where in the hell—"

Claire lifts her head and turns toward us.

"Oh fuck!" I yell. Claire screams and starts beating her fists against the wheel. I grab for her. She thrashes about wildly.

Blood begins to run at the corner of her mouth. One eye is completely swollen shut. She wears only a torn blouse. The air is filled with the smell of semen and blood. Gwen is frozen. I am holding Claire while she lurches forward in deep sobs. I rock her back and forth. I don't say anything.

"Gwen, go get a blanket," I whisper. Gwen runs toward the barracks.

"GET TOP TOO!"

Her careless bounce when she walks has smoothed out, but it's still there. In her hand a plastic bag with a tag fastened to it. As she gets closer, her eye clearly reminds me of the violence she endured. It is turning that awful yellow, and the welling is now subsiding. Above the eyebrow, a small bandage covers the stitches that are to be removed in a day or so.

"Hi." I smile at her. "You okay?"

She shakes her head and pushes the plastic bag in my hand. Large red letters on the tag stand out: **EVIDENCE, Personal Property—Berger, C.**

Claire steps off the sidewalk and sits down on the grass; she rests her head in her hands with elbows on bended knees. I sit down beside her. She looks at me with tears streaming down her face.

"It was awful . . . ," she stammers telling me. Today was her lie detector test. The JAG officer appointed to help her, told her it would strengthen her case since the scum who raped her refused to take one. He claimed Claire instigated the sex and got scared after the fact, panicked.

"It's over. Done with," she blurts out.

"What do you mean? They gonna throw his ass in jail?"

"No!" Silence.

"Well, Jesus, Claire, what do you mean it's over with?"

"His commander. Says he's too good of an NCO. Oh, Gail, I just can't do it, I feel so humiliated. Maybe it was my fault?"

"Shit, Claire, that's a Goddamn lie, and you know it."

Claire gets up and brushes her hands, turns, bows her head, and begins to walk toward the barracks."

"Come on, Gail. I don't want to talk about it."

"But, Claire—"

She glares at me. "I said I don't want to talk about it!"

We walk in silence to the barracks. Inside, Claire looks at me.

"I want to be alone for a while."

"Claire, please, I need to be with you. I'll give you space—honest."

She touches my arm and smiles. We walk down the hallway.

"Gwen, you sit up front." I whisper.

She nods. Claire walks beside us. Today Gwen and I finally convinced Claire to go with us to the drive-in. For weeks Claire has avoided the car. When it was her turn to use it, she simply said she didn't feel like going anywhere.

Gwen and I had gone out and bought some terry cloth covers to put over the seats. We bought new floor mats and scrubbed it down with Pinesol. On the dashboard, a small dent caused by the struggle, couldn't be gotten rid of. We put a sticker and hung a smelly skunk in hopes of hiding the ugly reminder.

At first, even Gwen and I weren't crazy about getting in the car. Our rides were short and silent. It was painfully clear to us that our weekend excursions have come to an abrupt end.

Claire stops. We both look at her. Her eyes are fixed on the car. Gwen opens the door. I start to walk to the driver's side but change my mind.

"I'll ride up front." Gwen pulls the passenger seat forward so Claire can enter.

Claire takes a step forward. "I can't." She closes her eyes and gulps. "I just can't." She whirls around.

"Oh, Claire." I take her in my arms. I can see the tears and anger in her eyes. "It's okay . . . you don't have to."

Suddenly she breaks away from my arms. She turns toward the car and frantically beats on top of the roof with closed fists. She is striking and striking.

"NO! NO! NO!" she screams after each blow.

Gwen and I each grab an arm. We try to hold her. Both of us are scared that she will hurt herself.

"Let me go! Goddamn it!" Claire thrashes around. She bolts off toward the barracks. Gwen starts to follow her. I reach out and hold Gwen's arm.

"We really can't cover it up." Gwen sighs and glances toward me. "White washing it won't take away the memories." She closes the door, pivots to the right, and angrily kicks the tire. "Fuckin bastard!"

We walk to a shady tree and sit down. Picking up small pieces of debris and tossing them, we remain silent.

Quietly, barely speaking out loud, Gwen says, "Guess we need to think about selling it."

I nod. I stand up and stretch out my hand, "Come on, Gwen, let's go check on Claire." She takes my hand, gets up. We both walk toward the building.

I had no intention of staying in the service. I volunteered to go to radio school to learn a trade. Didn't think there was much demand on the outside for a third trombonist.

Gwen left for France, and Claire had gotten out of the service. We all vowed to stay in touch, and Gwen and I knew we had some lonely times ahead.

Fort Gordon Georgia was a big sprawling military installation right smack dab in the middle of the Georgia red mud.

"Wait, damn it," I curse trying to sneak the needle nose pliers around the drain. "Don't flush until I get this wire mesh over the drain."

The first sergeant just looked at me and shook her head. She told me that she had been here for three years and never had anyone asked if they could put flowers in the barracks . . . latrine specifically.

Our barracks were the old WWII wooden buildings. You didn't need windows. You could look through the cracks in the boards. The latrines had a series of old aluminum trough urinals, winding around the walls like drain pipes on a roof. Sixteen immaculate white porcelain toilets formed a perfect U and three stairs descended right in the middle of the U. It was a frightening prospect to think that while doing something so personal as shitting, someone might descend the stairs right in the middle of a good resounding fart. I sincerely believe here are a lot of constipated Signal WAC Trainees running around. Thank God the school toilets are a lot more private.

Mercedes and I have taken up a collection for soil and plants. We decided on geraniums—the hanging type mixed in with spider plants and Wandering Jew. Our first experiment had proved to be disastrous. We did a test run of two plants. We carefully placed soil and plants in the troughs. The drains were too big. The soil washed down the drain on the first flush. Going back to the drawing board, Mercedes came up with the idea to put pieces of old screen door wire over the drain, set gravel over the wire and then the soil. It worked!

"You know what, Gail"—Mercedes cocks her head sideways looking at the urinal troughs—"this must have been a barracks for giants."

I scowl as I look at her. "What the hell you talking about?"

"These damn urinals are as high as my boobs," she says with a straight face. "These guys had to be tall to pee here."

"You're just short. Who knows"—I wink at her—"maybe the army teaches the guys to pee up hill."

We work diligently, placing the wire mesh over the drain, setting the soil, and carefully place the plants for "maximum" effect. Finished, it gives our place a little class.

Radio school was over. The geraniums were still growing when I left Fort Gordon. I went one last time to flush the urinal, and then I left for Fort Myer, Virginia.

The leaf swirls around, rocks back and forth, rises, then dives, floats, and finally hits the windshield of the car. It slides down the glass and falls off out of sight. I sit in the car with my head in my hand, my elbow resting on the armrest.

Samuel, Shelley, and June enter the large white double doors and disappear. This is the fifth church we've been to. Hopefully we can get this ceremony over with. It started out exciting trying to find a preacher that would marry Shelley and Samuel. Most of the clergymen wanted them to be members of the faith—at least.

My brother Samuel had joined the navy; and three months previous, while he was visiting me with one of his Navy buddies, I had introduced Shelley to him. Now here they are getting ready to take the big leap. Samuel, who wouldn't say shit if he had a whole mouth full, finally got up the nerve to ask her to marry him.

June's carrot top head peers outside the church, making a strange contrast against the white backdrop of the white doors. She motions for me to come inside. The preacher must have said he would do it. Shutting the door of the car, I take the toe of my shoe and stir up a small pile of leaves. I proceed up the steps two at a time, stop, look around to see if anyone is near, and then one at a time I finish the climb.

I enter the back suddenly realizing I forgot to see what denomination the church is. It is unsettling for me to be inside. I keep thinking I should be more humble. I really do think the roof might cave in. On the rare occasions when I feel moved to pray, I ask God to forgive me if he can, and if anyone should be punished for things between Gwen and me, He should seriously consider dumping the burden on me.

I look where June is sitting on the front row. Samuel and Shelley are nowhere to be seen. The altar area is simple and plain. A white wooden cross covers the back wall. Fall flowers decorate the area with wonderful yellows, oranges, and gold. The thought rushes like a gale wind. I wonder if God loves queers. I quickly glance toward the roof. I silently make my way to where June is sitting, pausing now and then to stroke the smooth back of the polished wooden pews. I sigh. June looks up and moves slightly to the right so I can sit down.

"They're in the parish room with the preacher," she whispers. I sit down.

I look at June, Shelley's best friend, sitting there, her hands carefully folded. The green sweater dress brings out the freckles on her arms and her face. I heard them giggling the night Samuel proposed to Shelley. She had run into the barracks and burst into June's cubicle to share her exciting news. It was then I knew my brother would marry Shelley. The state of Virginia needed two witnesses; Samuel had asked me to be one of them. June was the other.

The door opens. Samuel and Shelley are holding hands. They move behind the black preacher as he heads toward the altar.

He looks toward June and me. "These your two witnesses?" Samuel nods.

"That's my sister," he beckons toward me, "and that's June."

The preacher extends his hand and shakes each of ours, one after the other.

"Reverend Grant." His warm voice is sincere.

He patiently instructs us where to stand and evokes a spiritual setting for the whole moment. The preacher's voice takes on a different texture as he begins the ceremony. The sound echoing throughout the empty church; it almost seems that there is another couple at the other end getting married.

"I now pronounce you man and wife," he ends the ritual.

Samuel's face gets red as his eyes quickly dart to each of us. He quickly bends down and kisses Shelley. He does not linger. The ceremony ended, Shelley and Samuel thank the preacher, and we move toward the door.

The air is fresh out here. It is easier to breathe. June is hugging Shelley. Samuel and I stand around, waiting.

We drive down the road looking for a restaurant. I wonder if the fifth restaurant will be the one to play host to our little wedding party. I turn around and watch out the back window as the little white church somewhere in Virginia fades out of sight. Damn, I think to myself, I still don't know what denomination that church is.

The phone crackles and pops. My heart is racing faster. "Gwen?"

"Gail?" she shouts.

"Gwen?" I cry, grinning from ear to ear. "Oh, Gwen, it's you, it's really you!"

"How are you?" The words seem flat.

"Okay!" I say as I begin to wrinkle my forehead. "Are you okay?"

"Fine," she pops back. "Can you meet me at McGuire on Thursday?"

"Are you coming back?" I ask with surprise. "So early?"

"Yes . . . I . . . we have to leave France," she stutters. "Can you meet me at McGuire or not?" Her last question seems bitter—insistent.

"Well, of course." Silence. "God! I will be glad to see you." I switch the phone receiver to the other ear. "Do you know when?"

"No," she says, "My flight number is R47MK."

"Gwen, I'll be there," I echo. "Why—." The click sounds extra loud as she hangs up.

DeGaulle has been busy kicking the American forces out of France.

The riverbank is steep as I climb down to my favorite rock. I look across the other side of the river and see the steeple of George Washington University. Sometimes I can hear the chimes in the distance. The rush of water around the rocks is like a metronome. "Dearest Gwen," I begin to write.

Now I get to see Gwen in less than one year instead of two.

I set the vase of roses on the badly chipped dresser. A six-pack of beer lies in the cooler. I give the room a quick once-over to make sure it is just perfect. I am not sure what I expected for a $12 motel room, but who cares what the room looks like.

The car rolls to a stop at the entrance gate to McGuire. Showing my ID card, I ask the guard the way to the passenger terminal.

"Go to the end of the street, take a left," he spits out the direction in robot fashion. "Park in marked areas only."

Walking into the terminal, I quickly glance at my watch. She might have already landed. I search the incoming flight board to see if her flight has arrived. Flight R47MK—landed.

I stop an airman with an armband marked Customs and ask him the way to the incoming flight area. He points in a straight-ahead fashion.

Thanking him, I turn my eyes, begin walking forward; and coming down the hall is Gwen. My heart will burst. She does not see me.

I look at her and see her body push against the uniform. DeGaulle had nothing to do with her early return.

We greet each other with polite excitement. Gwen does not hug me or shake my hand.

Her eyes caste down, she whispers, "Thanks for coming." She looks up at me, tears streaming down her face. "I am sorry. Truly."

The ride back is silent. Opening the motel room door, the smell of roses fills the air.

Closing the door, I quickly take a beer from the cooler, turn to her and ask, "Why?"

"Because I was lonely."

My transfer came through. I had waited only six months. I reported to Fort Meade, Maryland. Gwen left without a word, and we never said good-bye. Someone told me later that she had had a baby girl.

The wad of paper falters then falls in the wastepaper basket. Two points! Lunchtime! I am glad to take a break, get away from this desk.

Through the door walks the sergeant major on his way to play cards with "the boys." He carries a magazine in his hand.

"Kmmmmm" I clear my throat. The big surly man sits behind his desk, his head bend down.

"Sit." He points to a chair without looking up. He puts down his pencil and turns his head toward me.

"PFC Westbrook-Sergeant Major," I offer.

"I know who you are." His eyes give no clue of what he is thinking. I twist in my seat and scratch my cheek with my index finger. Silence.

"Do your job and stay out of my way, Westbrook. We'll get along fine." he abruptly proceeds. "I don't like WACs. You're a WAC, so I don't like you."

Is this guy for real? Neanderthal!

As the sergeant major passes by, he tosses the magazine on my desk.

"Here, Westbrook. Go look at the pictures."

I look at the cover. *Playboy.* Bastard!

"Hey, Gail!" a strange voice echoes.

I open one eye, focusing on the faint light coming through the curtain of my cubicle. A shadowy figure is bent near me.

"Who the hell is there?" I growl.

"It's me Esther," she says. "Hurry! There's some dude down at the other end of the bay."

"What?" I sit up in bed. "What's he doing in here?"

"Must've come over from the stockade." Her words fade as she heads toward the front. "Jesus! Shut up and come on. They're gonna kill the poor bastard."

I throw the covers back and grab my robe and slide into my thongs. The last guy that scaled the stockade walls and tried to climb in our barracks lost his footing on the second-floor balcony and fell—broke his leg. He had just walked away from the stockade without being noticed. Wonder how this one got out.

Walking out my cubicle, I turn and retrieve my flashlight. My thongs flap lightly on the floor

"Keep the Goddamn noise down" comes an unfriendly grunt.

Esther is one of the young privates in the bay and is a few paces in front of me. She turns to see if I am following. Within seconds we are at the end of the bay, near the fire exit.

Huddled in a corner is a fatigue-clad soldier; his hands covering the top of his head. There is an angry silence. One hand is bloody, and blood trickles down the side of his head. Around him are five or six women all holding high heels by the toe. The heels held back ready to strike if he moves.

The assistant barrack sergeant, Jean, sees me. She looks toward him and then returns her glance to me.

"Bastard was knelt down touching one of the troops on the arm," she hisses.

"She okay?" I scan around for the troop. "Where is she?"

"She went to get Top."

There is movement from the soldier. The women begin to move in closer, cocking back their hands with the heels. The soldier clears his throat.

"Hey, lady . . . ," he squeaks.

"Shut up, Fuck Face," barks Jean, "or we'll go another round."

I gesture with my hands to calm down. I shake my head wondering how all this happened and I didn't hear a sound.

As if hearing my thoughts, Jean explains that the guy panicked when the young troop sat up suddenly with a heel that she had silently taken from under the bed shoe display and clubbed him one. He darted out of the cubicle, ran into Jean, stumbled, and fell. The other young troop was right behind him and events just took over from there.

I hear footsteps. Turning around I see Top with an MP. She smiles and shakes her head.

"You, women, are something," she says.

The MP approaches the soldier, handcuffs him, and carries him off.

"Okay, everybody down to the orderly room," commands Top. "The action is over. Now starts the paperwork."

Momentarily, there is only Top and I. All the other women have ducked into their cubicles and put their heels back into their shoe alignment under their bed. We turn and walk down the bay hallway.

The road curves and switches back as we make our way down off the Blue Ridge Parkway. I glance in the mirror, quickly surveying my passengers. Some passengers are sleeping. A few are quietly engaged in conversations. Others are looking out the window enjoying the signs of an early summer. I like driving the bus for unit outings. A few people are noticeably missing. Nita told me it was best that she didn't come.

The smoke from the grill changes direction, and it seems everyone moves with it. Elaine and Nita open another beer. Laughter follows as the beer squirts all over Joyce. Nita glances in my direction, and then quickly looks away. I throw the rubber ball toward Nita as Tandy her dog leaps and bounds after it. Nita grabs the ball and keeps it.

"Lie down, Tandy," Nita commands. Tandy throws back her ears and with a big sigh flops down beside Nita's foot.

I walk to where the three are sitting. It seems to be quieter. It is uncomfortable being here. Aw just my imagination, I scold myself.

"Hi," I greet them. Elaine nods. Nita takes a drink of her beer, and Joyce reaches and pats Tandy's head. It is silent.

"Well, guess I'll grab me something to eat." It takes all my will power to keep from running.

I walk from group to group, exchanging greetings and shoptalk. Pausing here and there to watch card games, backgammon games, or cribbage challenges. Making my way to the grill, I grab a hamburger and find my way to an isolated corner. I can't figure Nita and why she is so strange. Every Since Joyce Anderson was assigned here there has been a noticeable change in Nita.

I half-finish the hamburger, toss it toward a nearby trash can. I lie back on the ground, crossing my feet at the ankle, and put my arm across my closed eyes. I let my mind wander where it may.

"Gail," comes the gravely voice. I remove my arm and squint in the bright sunlight. It's Elaine. "Mind if I sit for a second."

I nod as I sit up Indian style.

"You okay?" she asks.

"Confused."

"You better talk to Nita," She glances around watchfully.

"Easier said than done," I throw out. "She's made it obvious she doesn't want to talk with me."

"Joyce's been talking to her."

"About what?" I scowl. I lean back and look directly at Elaine.

"Don't be coy, Gail," she hisses. "You know damn well what about."

I stretch and rub the back of my neck, trying to make it look natural while I steal a peek where Nita and Joyce are sitting. They are gone!

"Really, Jody." I speak quietly using Elaine's nickname. "I don't even know Joyce that well." I grab a handful of grass and toss it toward on invisible target. "I saw her a couple of times at Fort Gordon."

"She told Nita you were a CID plant."

"She told her WHAT?"

"You heard me."

"Bullshit! Where in the hell did she get that nonsense?" I shake my head and roll my eyes in the back of my head. The Criminal Investigation Division of the Army was everywhere. They loved a witch-hunt.

"Said you worked with CID after you finished radio school."

"Oh my god," I chuckle. "First Sergeant asked me if I wanted to do role-playing for the interrogators at the MP School."

"Did you?"

"Well . . . ya," I say with disbelief. "But Christ, I'm sure as hell not in cahoots with that outfit." I shrug my shoulders and throw up my hands. "It . . . it was something to do until I got my assignment orders . . . for Christ's sake."

"Like I said . . . you better talk to Nita." Elaine gets up and walks away.

I sit here stunned, shaking my head, not believing our conversation. It is beyond me why Joyce would want to say something like that . . . unless? I jump up as I see Joyce heading for her car. I don't see Nita.

Nita's door is closed. I knock lightly.

"Come in," she calls out. I enter. She is standing before her refrigerator door. "Oh, it's you."

"What does that mean?" I ask as I close the door quietly behind me. I move close to where she is standing. She backs away.

"Nothing," she coldly answers. She takes a cigarette from her coffee table and lights it.

"Can I sit down?" I ask.

She nods. "What was Jody talking to you about?" She takes a long drag of her cigarette and slowly blows the smoke through her nose.

"About me working with the CID." She stops blowing the smoke from her nose in midstream, then finishes.

"She didn't waste time, did she?" she states sarcastically. "And what was your answer?"

"It's bullshit, Nita." I raise my voice. "A fuckin' lie. Who the hell does this Joyce think she is?"

"A friend." She throws up her arms. "Listen, this is no place to talk."

"But—"

"We need to cool it for a while," she says in a dark whisper.

"Won't you give me a chance to explain?" I ask in desperation.

"Later," her voice growing stern. "I think you'd better go."

"Nita . . . please."

She opens the door. Looks at me and says, "Thanks for stopping by."

It is dark as we approach the main gate. I brake and watch carefully as the MP waves us through. It's only five minutes from there to the WAC Detachment.

I roll to a stop in the parking lot behind the building. "Everybody, be sure to take all your stuff with you," I call out as they rise to exit the bus.

A few minutes later, I am on the way to the motor pool to clean the bus and turn it in.

As I check the oil and fill the bus up with gas, I decide to run by the NCO barracks and see if Nita is still up. Maybe I can get her to go have a cup of coffee and talk.

Finished.

I jump in my car and swing by her building. Her car is gone. I suppose she went to Delaware. I look in the direction of Joyce's room. Her car is there, but her room is dark.

I take the stairs halfheartedly two at a time. I am tired, and a nice hot shower will feel good. I quickly throw my clothes off, put on my robe, and head for the latrine. Standing under the shower, I force all thoughts of Nita under the surface. I just want to relax without thinking.

I float off to sleep. Weaving in and out of a maze, soft strokes on my arms.

"Specialist Westbrook" comes a whisper. I keep hearing my name like way off in the distance. "Specialist Westbrook." It comes again.

I open my eyes. It's the charge of quarters. "You got a phone call. It's your brother."

I shake my head, trying to focus on the moment. I grab my watch. "What time is it?" I ask.

"Three . . . in the morning."

"Okay," I yawn. "I'm coming." I once again grab my robe and sleepily make my way downstairs to the charge of quarters Room.

The first sergeant is standing there. I look at her suspiciously. She then touches my shoulder. Brother, three o'clock . . . first sergeant. I desperately grab the phone.

"Chris?" I ask.

"Gail Ann," he starts.

"What is it, Chris?" I demand. "What's wrong?"

"I'm sorry, Gail Ann . . . Mom's dead."

"No!" I drop the phone and walk out.

The flight home is a blur. After landing in Cheyenne, I catch a bus to Sinclair Wyoming. Home to bury my mother.

The door slams shut. Mother's presence hangs heavy in this car. I touch the steering wheel.

Her dark green and gray eyes check the back mirror. She glances to the right and left. She splays her hands and then full grips the steering wheel. The young boys in the car next to us have baited her to drag when the light turns green. Old woman is written on their faces. She revs the motor. My mother the hot rodder. I look at

her feet; a perfect blend of clutch and accelerator is waiting for the
right moment. The light flickers and green! The young boy peels
and squeals, fishtailing before us. Mom leans back in the seat and
accelerates slowly. The mischief fills her eyes, her eyebrow slightly
rising. She chuckles, "Wasn't very nice, huh?"

The motor springs to life at a turn of the key. I back the car down the driveway. The red brick house is shrinking in the background. I expect her any minute to walk out on the porch. She'll never come out.

The trees lining the street whoosh by as I drive toward the main road. The refinery, like a spider, branches its web over the tiny cluster of houses. It is an oasis in a wasteland; a cross in a cemetery.

She lay quietly in the backseat. The pain gripping her body, but
she was bored. She wanted to go to Yellowstone. In twenty minutes
we had piled our stuff in the car, and we took off. She looked at me
in the mirror.
"I just don't want to die alone," she whispered.

I clench my hand and hit the steering wheel with my fist. I don't want to remember. Damn it! Goddamn it Mom! Why did you have to say that? Shit, I wasn't here. FUCK IT! FUCK YOU, GOD!

I take a deep breath and sigh. I look at my watch. Marie will be at the train station in another twenty minutes. I haven't seen her in over ten years. I look out the back window. The dust sprays behind the car as I turn off toward the station. I stop the car. I sit and look around. There is no one.

Getting out of the car, I kick a stone and flinch as it hits the side of the sandstone structure. I slam my hands into my jeans pocket. Hunching my shoulders, I walk the long way around the station. I don't want to talk to anyone. The wind blows a weed in the distance. It tumbles and stops alongside the track. Caught! I glance down the track. It stretches forever, coming to a point in the far distance.

In just a short distance along the horizon, the train moves like an ant. Progressively getting larger. The dock is still empty, must be no others coming or going. The train slows; the brakes begin to screech! It stops. I look left and right as the silver cars gleam against the bright Wyoming sun.

To the left is movement. A black man in a blue cap swings a step out. I turn. He extends his hand out. Another hand meets his. Aunt Marie steps down and turns toward me. In her hand a small handbag. It's Mom with gray hair. But . . . but Mom is dead!!!

Marie smiles. "Gail Ann! What are you doing? . . . Where's Ruth?" I cannot answer her. I hear her gasp for air.

"Oh God! NO!" she cries. I take her in my arms.

Irises cover the polished gray metal coffin. The ribbon flutters slightly in the cool breeze. I sit here. The closed coffin allows no one a final glimpse. She lay dead for twenty-four hours before anyone found her. Except for Doris, one of our neighbors, who hadn't seen her pick up the mail, she might have lain there longer. It was 102 degrees in the house when the town sheriff and Doris broke in. Dad had been in Montana, working. Fuckin' bastard was screwing some broad my age.

Big brother Chris told me the coroner wouldn't allow me to see her. I believed him. Now it was too late. Bullying me again, the bastard. I allowed it.

In my mind's eye I see her lying there not moving and not breathing. I never thought Mom would ever die. I keep thinking of the tiny canister beside her, surrounded in the dark soft cushions of the coffin. Samuel told me that Mom had hidden the ashes of Robert Glenn, the brother I never knew—died before I was born—all these years and now they would both be put to rest. No one knew that, except us three kids and big brother didn't know that I had been told.

Over the top of the coffin, in the background, are red felt curtains stretching the length of the wall. Behind that, the baptismal bath Mom and I shared that Sunday afternoon nine years before. I had gone with her because she didn't want to go alone. I realize now it was one of her many acts of trying to find peace to give a sense of purpose to her life.

I can hear the strains of music. Samuel, Paul, and Mary's **"Blowin in the Wind."** The song I chose. Mom's favorite.

The preacher is beginning his eulogy. I do not listen. I think that his words will be superficial—they are meant to heal and right now I do not want to heal. I am angry and hurt that we did not say good-bye. I am the same age she was when I was growing inside of her.

I turn and look at Samuel, the quiet one, and I grieve for him.

It is time to go. The pallbearers are taking the coffin down the aisle. We all follow. Somewhere in all of this, I am trying to make sense of it.

The miles to the graveyard pass by like the frames in a movie. The sagebrush stretches forever all around. In the foreground, the arch to the graveyard looks like a door to another world. We pass through, and my life changes forever.

The mound of dirt alongside the grave is covered with artificial grass; the hearse is parked, and the doors to the back are opened. They have put Mom on the portal that will lower her down. I start to cry for the first time.

*   *   *

The pale mint-colored car drives up and parks in the nearly empty lot of the Fort Meade WAC Detachment. The unmarked car looks more military than a regularly marked motor pool vehicle.

Almost simultaneously, the car door swings open and the "twin" well-dressed men with highly polished shoes, argyle socks, short, well-groomed hair and matching suits with dark ties, step from the car. Both are wearing sunglasses; one takes them off, the other quickly follows suit. I watch them from the orderly room window as they slowly and deliberately walk across the parking lot. The stout one looks at me watching them, slips on his sunglasses once again and continues his slow purposeful gait.

As soon as they have hit the stairs to enter the detachment, I turn and make my way to the desk. Picking up a pencil, I move forward in my chair, begin to write with a pretense for work and wait for "Uncle CID" to appear. As if on cue, they enter the room.

"May I help you?" I ask looking up. Both reach inside their jacket pocket and pull out the familiar black ID wallet and flip it open.

"Agent Anderson," he smiles, "and this is Agent Kennedy."

I say nothing. The silence is uncomfortable as I look at them. First Sergeant Tizzard steps into the room and introduces herself. They follow her into the commander's office. The door is pulled to, a last final click as someone gives it an extra pull.

An hour passes by and still the door is closed. Occasionally we hear a cough or the scraping of a chair. Business is traditionally slow this time in the afternoon. Few phone calls, but the constant shuffling of paper never stops. Vera and I look at each other wondering what comes next. This is a waiting game.

An hour and a half later, they emerge with Agent Kennedy giving a "thanks for your cooperation" good-bye. Top's face is flushed, obviously pissed with something. She waits till the car is gone from the parking lot. She looks at me and with controlled coolness, walks into Captain Garrett, the Company Commander's, Office once again and slams the door shut.

This time it is not quiet. Her loud voice carries through the door, and Vera and I are no longer wondering what's next.

"CPT Garrett, this is also my detachment!" comes her angry voice. "This detachment has just been through a shitty witch hunt."

Vera and I listen and then I get up and close the door to the orderly room and turn the lock. Top reminds the captain how we all suffered as we saw our first sergeant and company commander relieved because of gossip, mistrust, and deception. Vera and I try to make busy work.

The tall agent stands at the other end of the table and stares at me.

"How often have you slept with a woman?"

"Never," I say as mental slides click in and out.

"Five, six, or so many times you can't count," he persists.

I remain silent.

"Have you ever been fist-fucked by a woman?" He tries to startle me.

Again I say nothing.

"You know Judy Taylor?" He watches me closely.

I nod.

"Then you know she is a homosexual," he emphasizes.

"Why would you think I know that?" I ask.

"Oh you can talk," he chides. "She mentioned you when we last talked with her." Silence. "Want to know what she said?"

"I am sure you'll tell me."

"When's the last time you said you slept with a woman," he asks again looking at this notepad lying on the table.

Fuckin' bastard trying to trap me.

"Are you finished with me?" I ask as I start to stand up.

"For now," he turns toward the door opens it, then glances back. "But we'll see each other again, Westbrook. I promise. You can't hide forever." He disappears behind the closed door.

His words echo in my mind as I walk out in the muggy hot weather.

The door to CPT Garrett's office bursts open, and Top stomps out toward her own office. Behind her comes the CPT, her eyes wide and saucer like, her face as red as a beet.

Uncle CID's first tactic has succeeded—divide the alliance.

I press on the doorbell. Probably should have called, but I wanted to get away from there as fast as I could.

Armload after armload of clothes I throw haphazardly in the car. The stairs creak and moan every time I go down them. Surprises me that someone doesn't stick out their head and tell me to be quiet. It's 11:30 at night. Finished, I walk by Nita's door, hesitate, touch the door with the tips of my fingers wishing that it could bring it all back. She has gone away for the weekend to Delaware—with Ski.

I press the doorbell again.

"Yeah, yeah," comes a muffled shout through the thick wood door. "I'm coming!"

The door flies open. My friend Sarin is an enormous woman, and she fills the doorway with ease. She peers into the dark night while turning on the light.

"Gail?" she wipes her eye with one hand and yawns. "What the hell you doin' here . . . at this time of night?"

"Sorry." I toss my car keys from hand to hand. "I . . . I just needed to go somewhere!"

A big smile spreads across her face. "Well, damn woman . . . don't just stand there, get your ass in here." She grabs my arm and pulls me in the house.

The living room is a series of overstuffed chairs and overstuffed couches. Throw rugs and wall-to-wall carpet. On the one coffee table is Sarin and Judy's latest puzzle half-finished. On the walls are shellacked puzzles, some mounted in frames, others simple finished products of their addictive hobby. In one corner is a jungle of plants of every variety and species that can live either without water or can live with excessive watering. Peeking out like a one-eyed monster is a "big screen" television.

She goes to a closet in the hallway and returns. Throwing a pillow and blanket toward me, she says, "We'll talk in the morning." She makes a sweeping gesture with her hand, "Pick wherever you want to crash."

I reach out and grab the pillow and blanket in midair. "Thanks."

"You got any pj's?"

"Out in the car."

"Wait!" she commands. She disappears once again and returns several minutes later. She hands me a T-shirt. "I put out a towel and new toothbrush in the bathroom . . . now good night."

"Good night," I call back. "Thanks!" I hold the T-shirt up. It's one of Sarin's. The front has a forlorn-looking frog sitting on a wilted lily pad and underneath is printed—*I'm so happy I could just shit!*

I throw a makeshift bed together on one of the couches and put the T-shirt on. It comes down to my knees.

Crawling under the blanket, I have no recollection of falling asleep.

"Aaaaaaaaaaaaaaaaaaaaaaaiiiiiiiiiiiiiiiiiiiiiiiieeeeeeeeeeeeeee!" The scream pierces my morning sleep. Judy tackles me on the couch and begins to tickle me unmercifully.

"Ohhhhhhhhhhh, shit," I laugh. "Judy, stop. Haaaaaaaaa, I'll pee my pants."

She stops, smiles, and then scoops me up in a warm bear hug.

"Hi, Gail," she says as she sits back on the couch. Sarin walks in the room carrying a large mug of coffee, hands it to me, and sits down.

I take a sip of the coffee. "Hmm, good." I look at Sarin. "But then you always made a good cup of coffee."

"Well?" She looks at me.

"Well what?" I ask.

"Shit, woman, you know damn well what?" Judy gets up and disappears in the kitchen and returns with a glass of orange juice.

"Not much to say." I put the coffee cup down on the table. "Nita left last night with Ski."

Sarin and Judy, both government employees, spend time with me talking about Nita and where I go from here. I had made it easy for Nita. I volunteered for recruiting duty, so I was on my way to school. Nita wouldn't have to see me mope around nor would I have to see her.

"I got just the thing for you, woman." Sarin lifts herself from the chair. "Misery loves company." She winks toward Judy. Judy smiles.

"I don't want no booze!" I emphasize looking at them both.

"Promise," Judy throws up her hands. "This is much better."

'Yeah," Sarin's whiskey tenor voice rolls the yeah in seductive honey as she bends down and squeezes my cheeks. "Sylvia!"

"Oh no ya don't!" I exclaim. Throwing Sarin's hands from my cheeks. "No . . . no and no."

"Too late," chides Judy, "she's coming over tonight for rummy."

We banter back and forth, knowing I can stay or leave. It's too early to report to Indiana, and I'm sure as hell not returning to Fort Meade. They can manipulate all they want, but they can't make me "drink the water." I decide I'll stay. I'll meet Sylvia. She too had recently ended a relationship—three years. Besides it'll keep my mind off Nita—maybe.

Sarin and Judy busy themselves around the house; I start to get dressed, but remember I left my stuff in the car. It is parked way down off Rock Creek Parkway. Judy reminds me that I left a pair of underpants and socks the last time I stayed. I use a sweatshirt and pair of slacks from her. We both are about the same build with some slight variations. After a shower maybe I'll go down and get my stuff out of the car.

We spend the afternoon building puzzles. In between interlocking pieces are short stabs of pain. I can't help wishing that relationships would be like puzzles—so many pieces, search for the right shape, and drop it in place. If it falls apart, pick it up, and put it back together. But somewhere I guess Nita and I lost one of the pieces.

The door bells rings. I look at my watch—five already. I hear a muffled greeting at the front door. Sarin returns, and if I could get my eyes off this woman's chest maybe I could give a proper greeting. I thought I had big boobs! But I am so out of proportion; this woman is perfectly balanced. She's a large woman with incredible boobs! The heat from my face makes me aware that I must be red as a beet. Judy taps me on the shoulder.

"Hi." I stick out my hand. Her hand, shaking mine, is like a fish that is cold and slips out quickly. I want to apologize for being so obvious, but I turn away instead. I get the feeling she wouldn't have come if she'd known I was here. Sarin and Judy games I guess.

We play rummy for a couple of hours, then Sarin and Judy go out to get some pizza, leaving Sylvia and me alone.

"Ah . . . Sylvia," I pretend to clean already clean fingernails, "I was a . . . a kind of rude when you came in . . . sorry."

"Yeah," she turns toward me, "They tend to get in the way of the big picture, don't they?" I flinch. She winks, and we both begin to laugh—endlessly.

"You know . . . mind if I bum one of your cigarettes?" She holds the pack in her hand. I shake my head.

"Help yourself," I return.

She lights her a cigarette, inhales, and continues. "You know this was arranged?" she states as she exhales.

"Na . . . they didn't know I was coming. I came without being invited."

"Sarin called me this morning at nine."

"Ohhh! Okay." I say nodding, remembering that Judy attacked me early this morning around 9:30.

We talk lots of small talk. Time passes by and with it Sylvia moves closer to me—or maybe I am moving closer to her.

"I miss being held," she blurts out.

"Wh . . . what?" I look at her with a slight scowl. Boy this room is stuffy. Wait a damn minute, what the hell am I doing?

"I miss being held," she whispers. She brings her arm around the back of the couch and rests her hand on my neck. Boy I really didn't notice how close she moved—or maybe she's got long arms. I look at her arms.

As fast as lightning, before I change my mind, I grab her in my arms and bury my face in those incredible breasts. And just as quickly, I jump back way to the end of the couch and gulp.

"Oh shit, Sylvia," I wrench my hands, then run my fingers through my hair. "I'm sorry . . . truly." I jump up from the couch and start searching for my pack of cigarettes.

"I am too," she holds the pack of cigarettes toward me, "that you left."

I take the cigarettes, but she doesn't let go; instead she stands up—she's several inches taller than I. It seems like the most natural thing that she would gather my head in her arms and draw me to her . . . just at the level where it is hard to see the big picture. It's burning between us, and there is no putting out the fire until the fire burns itself out.

If Judy and Sarin returned, I would have never noticed and neither would Sylvia.

"I should feel guilty." I turn my head and look at her lying beside me.

She raises up on one elbow, resting her head in her hand. "Why?"

Somehow we had managed to move from Sarin and Judy's living room to the den toward the back of the house. The big oval rug had served as our bed. I play with a string, twisting it around and around my forefinger. I am conscious that her breast lay soft against my other arm. I don't move.

"Because . . . because I used you." I look toward the ceiling, counting the dark squares in the design of the overhead light.

"Then I used you," she traces the profile of my forehead to my chin—and back again. "I won't feel guilty"—she brushes her lips against my cheek—"because it's nice."

I close my eyes and suddenly realize that there are tears, and they run down my face and spill on the rug. She wipes them gently away, then quietly gathers me to her and lies back. My head rests against her shoulder. She tenderly rocks me back and forth, and I am grateful to this woman. I return her embrace.

We move into the night and greet the day, between sleep and making love.

"Smell that," she whispers.

I nod.

"Coffee!!" she shouts throwing back the skimpy blanket and sitting up. "Oh shit! My back!" She laughs as she arches and puts her hands against the small of her back.

"The floor is hard huh!" I roll to the side, get up on my hands and knees, and place my foot on the floor, lifting myself to stand up. Groaning all the while.

"Damn," she curses.

"What happened?" I look at her with concern.

"Our clothes . . ."

"Crap . . . they're in the living room." I wink at her.

We move together and wrap the blanket around us. Laughing, we move through the house toward the living room.

Sarin sees us and with a big guffaw, "Hey Judy, I told you we had company . . . somewhere."

We all are laughing. I give Sylvia an extra hug as we make our way to get our clothes. She feels nice, this compassionate woman.

I pick up the telephone receiver and begin to dial the number. Pissed because I left my training records behind. Best call the company and get them to forward the records to Fort Ben Harrison, Indiana.

The telephone rings for the third time.

"WAC Company, Specialist Banks" comes Vera's pleasant voice.

"Vera, this is Sergeant Westbrook."

"Sergeant Westbrook!" comes the excited voice. "Hold on . . . don't hang up!"

A muffled sound followed by the sound of someone clearing their throat.

"Westbrook?" comes the voice. "This is First Sergeant Tizzard."

"Top?" I ask confused. I look toward Sylvia who is sitting across from me in the other chair. I shrug my shoulders.

"Where in the hell are you?" Top demands. "Are you okay?"

"Sure," I say suspiciously. "Why do you ask?"

"When's the last time you were near your car?"

"Couple of days." Anger is rising in my voice. "Top, what the hell is going on?"

"You get your butt down to the nearest police station," she commands. "Police are looking for you! Then you call me back." There is a loud clunk and then silence. She hangs up. Damn! No explanation—just hangs up!

I replace the receiver. What the hell is going on?

Jesus, I should have gone to the car a long time ago. Better call the police—no I'll go check the car and then go down to the station.

"Come on, Sylvia," I say as I grab my keys off the coffee table. "Something's happened to my car."

"Where's it at?"

"Just off Rock Creek Parkway."

"My god! Way down there!" she says with disbelief. "Let's go in mine."

"Let's walk then we can drive mine back." I head toward the front door.

We walk with a brisk pace, the eight or nine blocks to Rock Creek. The night I had come to Sarin and Judy's place I had wanted to walk and think. I parked and headed out toward their house.

As we approach my car, it doesn't look any different. The doors are closed; I can see no bumps and scrapes. The clothes are still piled in the backseat. I wonder what Top meant.

Sylvia puts her hands to the back window on the driver's side and peers in while I take the key to unlock the door.

A nearby policeman approaches me and asks if that is my car and I explain that I am the owner of the car. He tells me I have some explaining to do. We go to the police station. Top's concern becomes realization as the police tell me that they found my car open and clothes strewn from one end of the parkway to the other. They had been watching the vehicle ever since then in hopes of either the driver or whoever might show up.

The desk sergeant gives me my keys back. He hands me a pink slip. Its a Goddamn parking ticket—illegal parking. Smiling, he calls one of the patrolmen to take us back to my car.

"Gail," says Sylvia as she gets into the car. "I'll say one thing: no one could accuse you of being boring."

We both laugh as I start up the car and take off to park in Sarin and Judy's driveway.

CHAPTER 8

Recruiting Duty

I had thirty days to report to Springfield, Massachusetts, after completing recruiting school. It was time to go home in Wyoming, to see my father, his new wife, and their new baby—my half sister?

The highway stretches out before me like a ribbon on wrapping paper. The wind is hot and dry. I look down at the speedometer—110 mph. Doesn't seem like it. The North Dakota scenery creeps by. Not a car in sight.

I am in Circle, Montana. Two years after Mom's death I am about to meet the woman who now occupies her space. I should say woman and child. My father did the "honorable" thing and married her when they learned she was pregnant. I didn't know they had gotten married until after she had had Katie. Samuel had casually mentioned it in one of his rare phone calls.

Main Street, abandoned. Western town. Closes down when the post office locks up. A neon light, Leona's, buzzes and sputters as the gases in the sign try to ignite. Several pickup trucks are parked outside. Most of them haven't been washed for weeks. The smell of dust and cut wheat fill the air. I pull up beside a motorcycle and stop the car. I need to find out where Dad lives.

I open the screen door. As I come in to the smoky room, I can see the backs of a dozen or so men seated at the bar. They all turn their heads around and look at me. Their faces

are brown and their foreheads are white where their hats had
been—"quart low on shit!" The Country and Western music
blares in the background. Off to the right is a pool table; two
players concentrating on the rolling, clicking balls. Behind
that is a table with chips and poker hands covering the top.

I'm not about to turn around and walk out. I walk up to
the bar. The bartender stands before me, his eyes looking
straight at me. He says nothing.

I swallow. "Ranch Road. How far?" I squeak.

"Up the road A block or so. By the John Deere Dealer."

I would have loved to order a beer, but I wasn't about to
drink one here. I had intruded on a sacred inner sanctum.
I raise my hand in a gesture of thanks and walk back toward
the door. I force myself not to run.

I take a deep breath of the cool evening air as I walk out.
My car is covered with a thin film of dust. Walking up to the
driver's side, I put my elbows over the door, resting my face
in my hands. Wonder what his reaction will be?

With the index finger of my right hand I artistically write
shit on the top of the car, then a smiley face. Sure would like
to have some coffee. I'll get some there. Turning around, I
lean my butt against the door. I fold my arms across my chest;
lay my head back, and close my eyes.

*Aunt Bev and Uncle Eddie are still asleep. Mom and Dad are
in Sonny's old bedroom. I open the door quietly. Are they asleep?
They are both sitting up in bed, naked. He has one breast in his
hand, and his mouth is sucking on her other breast. Mom's head
is thrown back; tears are rolling down her face. I cannot take my
eyes away. How can she let him do that? I drop my eyes and silently
shut the door.*

Okay, Gail! Let's get this the fuck over with!

Ranch Road, just like ole "friendly" bartender said. House
fits the name of the street. I pull in the driveway. Dad's Chevy

pickup parked. Shiny. He never let it get dirty; if it was, he washed it even if it was raining.

I ring the doorbell.

"Door's open!"

I walk in, guessing my way, looking in each room as I walk down the hallway. A light at the end suggests that's where he is at. At the door way I see Dad, his back toward me. He is bending over picking up something from the floor.

"Traci?" he mumbles.

"Nope." I am looking into the eyes of a blue-eyed light-haired living picture of myself. Katie is looking straight at me. She is sitting in a high chair waving her arms around, above her head a spoonful of some unknown substance about to be flung at Dad.

Thock! With a gleeful sound from Katie, the glob has found its mark. Dad's balding head is covered with a gooey mess.

"Shit!" he grumbles. He turns as he puts his hand to his head and sees me.

"It's you!" he says. "I thought you were Traci."

"Hi, Dad." I am trying not to laugh.

"Why in the hell didn't you call you were coming?"

If it weren't so Goddamn far out in the boondocks, I'd let the door hit me in the ass as I walked out. Fuck!

"Sorry!" I explain to him it was spur-of-the-moment decision that I wanted to surprise him.

He begins to clean up the mess. I look at him. His chest has slipped around his waist. I'm looking around for wonder woman. As though he reads my thoughts. "Traci's out driving combine. Should be home soon."

Light is reflected as a car pulls up in the driveway. A dull thump as a car door closes. Footsteps. The front door opens.

Down the hallway walks the best-looking butch I ever saw.

Dust flies in great clouds as we make our way across the rough sagebrush prairie. Quiet and serious, Traci does not smile or speak.

My Aunt Jean looks toward me and smiles. "Well, she certainly isn't Ruth, is she?"

The Stetson hat fits Traci like a glove. She looks at me looking at her.

"You comparing me too." Silence. "Well?"

"Yes, I suppose I am."

"And?"

"Honestly?"

She nods.

"No comparison. And unfair."

"It was a mistake, you know."

"What?"

"Marrying your father. If I hadn't been pregnant, I would have never done it."

She returns to her silence. Her eyes constantly survey the horizon. We make wide lazy circles and crisscross figures in the dry earth.

She slams on the brakes. The pickup goes into a sideways skid as she jerks the steering wheel right. In one motion, she pushes the door open while grabbing the .22 rifle mounted on the gun rack in the back window. Scrambling from the front seat, she plants her feet shoulder width, raises the rifle, aims, and squeezes the trigger. There is a loud explosion. Silence. She lowers her rifle.

In the near distance, I see the tiny prairie dog kick once or twice. Stiffen. Its is head missing.

She turns toward me. Holds the rifle out. "You wanna try."

I shake my head.

"No stomach for it?"

"No purpose."

"They're pests."

"To whom?"

In a split second, she whirls about raising the rifle once more to her shoulder, having caught the movement in her peripheral vision. Another prairie dog is dashing across the desert. Crack! Once again the rifle explodes. In slow motion the animal is severed in half before my eyes.

"Stop!!" I shout.

She lowers the rifle. Returning to the pickup, she places the gun back on the gun rack. Climbs in, slams the door shut. Throws the gear shift in low and peels off. Rooster tails of dirt and dust spray behind us.

I lean my head against the back of the pickup; beads of sweat roll off my forehead. I close my eyes. I will be glad to leave tomorrow.

We aren't supposed to take on a second job. It didn't look right for someone on recruiting duty to be working part-time. It might give the impression that the army didn't pay enough. Well it was the right thing to do. I had too much month at the end of my money.

Here I am, an assistant manager for Cumberland Farms and I have been on the job for about two months.

I ring up the items on the cash register. I smile at her, and she smiles back.

"You making a meatloaf?" I ask.

"Yep. How did you know?"

"You put in it everything I usually do," I say. "Besides this is the second time you've been here, can't help but notice."

She laughs and walks toward the door.

"Least ya could do is bring me a sandwich," I say, half-joking.

It's seven o'clock, time to lock the door. I close the cash register and walk around the counter to the door.

Just as I turn the key, I look up and she is standing there smiling, holding a meatloaf sandwich in her hand.

Ansi and I become fast friends.

I look out the huge glass windows, off to the right is a small organic garden. The tomatoes are succulent and turning red, almost ready to eat. Nearby, the corn with tassels serves as a reminder that the ears are ready to pick. At the edge of the garden, the green tops of the onions have been broken. It's only a matter of time before they are taken from the earth. I scan the area then do a retake as I see the top of an onion in the middle of the tomatoes. "An onion in a tomato patch," rather what I am with strangers like Jan and Lee.

I turn slightly toward the north wall and look at the wonderful stone fireplace that Ansi's friends have built. A fire crackles and pops breaking the silence of the late fall afternoon. Most of the house they built together with little outside help, except where law required they use licensed electricians and plumbers. I envy such ambition or maybe the roots they have.

I turn once again and look out the window, where far off toward the southwest a thunderstorm is rolling along the horizon. It melts into broken puffy gray clouds. Rays of sunlight pierce through the clouds like swords plunging to the earth. It's three-dimensional. It's being on the outside looking in.

They have been polite and warm; asking all the right questions and trying to make me feel comfortable. How did they meet? Suppose I'll never know, not that it makes any difference.

Nicole, the nurse recruiter, had invited me over for dinner. Really it was to meet her new friend Doreen. Nicole had told me about her with a twinkle in her eye.

The soft white couch swallows Doreen. She is a slight woman in her middle fifties with unforgettable gray/green eyes. Her hand and arm are carelessly flung over the back of the couch. Her thick hair peppered with streaks of gray frames her oval-shaped face. She smiles.

She had remained seated as I entered the room with Nicole. Nicole went directly behind Doreen, putting her hands on her shoulders and introduced us. She does it so naturally the flush rises to my face. Can they see?

Doreen is like a magnet; an unseen force draws me to her. I don't know this woman but somehow I can't help but like her. Her leg is resting half on half off the couch; the steel brace keeps it slightly bent. She puts her leg down to reach for my hand. The hinges on the brace squeak.

"Just call me Rusty." She winks. I smile then flinch slightly, wondering if I may have offended her.

The smoky bar on the side street always smells like a mushroom cellar. The parking lot was empty, and I am surprised so many women are here. Picnic tables used inside the bar are partially covered with red-and-white checkered tablecloths. The wet rings from sweating beer bottles glisten in the dim light. Peering into the darkness, I recognize Peggy.

Peggy is like a butterfly, going from table to table. Staying awhile, just long enough to let everyone know that she is here and to miss her when she leaves.

In the corner, a blonde with deep blue eyes watches her with a steely coldness. Before her are several empty beer bottles lined up in row.

A slow dance begins to play. I sit down at a nearly empty table and watch as the blonde gets up, hitting the table with her knee. The beer bottles rock precariously. She curses under her breath and grabs her knee. Peggy turns and looks in her direction, hesitates then heads out for another table.

Crossing the floor, with her thumbs hooked in the pockets of her pants, the blonde reaches out and grabs Peggy, turns her around and takes her in her arms. They begin to dance—slowly and stiffly. A slight movement tells me that Peggy is offering some resistance. The blonde's hands show white knuckles as she squeezes a reluctant hand.

Peggy's hand rests at shoulder level on the blonde. As they dance longer, each movement becomes more seductive. Peggy's hand has moved to the back of the blond's head, the thumb just behind the ear near the ear lobe, gently drawing tiny circles. Her eyes are closed.

I cast my eyes downward as I realize that my heart seems to beat quickly. A quick stab of pleasure shoots across me.

I raise my hand and motion for a beer.

Ansi is kissing her friend Linda, and I am uncomfortable. I wonder if what's her name—Florrie, I think—is as embarrassed as I am. I look across the motel room and see her sitting there. I do not notice any particular expression on her face. Maybe she is used to this.

Perhaps I should ask if she wants to go get a drink at the bar. Jesus, this is awkward. I wonder if Florrie know this is another of Ansi's eternal tries at matchmaking. She must have, otherwise how would Ansi have convinced her to come to the motel room and meet me? On the other hand, Ansi told me that Florrie was going to meet her and Linda at the Holiday Inn just off of Interstate 5 at the Rochester exit.

I get up and walk over to Florrie. Ansi and Linda are still kissing.

"Hey Florrie, how about we go get a drink down at the lounge?" I ask while motioning with my hand, "It's a . . . a . . . well hell, I feel like a fifth wheel in this room."

She laughs like a waterfall. She stands up. She is my height. Green eyes, small mouth, nice smile. I open the door, and she goes ahead of me. I look at her ass, cute. Crap, Gail you are disgusting. I chastise myself.

We walk down the corridor, the deep plush multicolored carpet absorbing the sound of our footsteps. I can't think of anything clever to say. I am at a loss to what to do next.

We get to the elevator. Florrie pushes the button. We wait. God, she must think I am a loser. I never could flirt, and older women just put me at a loss.

We both look up at the numbers over the elevator door and wait. We look at each other. Florrie begins to laugh. It is infectious and I begin to laugh. The door to the elevator opens; an elderly couple stand before us. We are still laughing. Looking at the expression on their faces, we both laugh harder. The couple begins to laugh. I am trying to say, "Excuse me." I lean against the door so it won't close. The couple leaves, laughing. Florrie enters laughing. I face the elevator directory and push the button marked lounge. The door closes. I turn around. She's right in front of me, as far away as the end of my nose. She kisses me.

Back in my room, we talked for hours establishing who we are and what we like. I want to go to this gentle woman and hold her, but I don't know what to do. I am scared. She has surrounded me with such good feelings. Like a melody you hear when watching the sun first come up.

"Come"—she pats the seat—"sit here beside me."

I walk with such coarse movements. I stand before her. She holds my hands for a moment, nothing more. Aware of only her, all other things come to a blur. I sit. She takes her hand and places it on my cheek. It is fire and ice. I have no strength to touch her—but oh God I want to. I am aware that she slides her hand from my check to elbow down to my hand, which she takes and brings to her lips. Her kiss burns through my palm.

I touch her jaw line; slide my fingertips down her neck, stopping just at the top of the first button. She sighs and lightly calls my name.

"You want to kiss me?" she whispers, waiting for no answer. "Then do."

I rise to kiss her. If only I can do it the way I want. I skim my lips over hers; I can't stay there long. I can't breathe. I keep drawing my breath in.

"Scared?"

I nod.

"Let me show you."

The long short journey begins. And I must be in a dream. She shows me without music what music sounds like. She takes the very essence of touch, gives it height and width and depth. She throws feeling against the wall, and we watch it shatter into little pieces before us. From that pile of broken pieces, she grabs passion and tenderness and stirs them in my heart. She shows me how to reach the top, but not spill over until we are both ready, until we have played the full strain. She also shows me that if we hit the wrong note, it's okay—that it's fun to start over again. She shows me how to capture moments in time that are there for the making.

In between, we sleep, sometimes apart, mostly together.

It is the YWCA in Rochester—of all the places to meet. I suppose Florrie just wants to make sure that I can afford it. Maybe she can't afford it. I have ached for her for a month now.

The rose lay on the pillow, a shallow reminder that Florrie had lain beside me. The smell of peppermint oil lingers long after she leaves. Pisses me off when I wake up and find her gone. Like a wisp of mist, she disappears; and I don't hear from her until she is ready for me. The telephone rings.

"Hello?"

"I'll call you," she whispers. The phone goes silent.

I glance at my watch. Seven. She should have been here a half hour ago. I grab the book out of my suitcase and throw myself on the bed. I toss the book back. Waiting.

There is a slight knock on the door. I try to walk to open it.

"Wait" comes her voice through the door. "Turn out the lights."

It's a hot day at Brighton Park. Florrie and I have been sitting here ready for over an hour. I look up at her. She winks back.

"Whew!" she puffs. "I'm hot!"

A book flies across the blanket. She puts her arms up over her head and grabs her shirt from the back and pulls it off. She is wearing no bra.

I shut off the light and open the door. She walks forward seductively, pushing me as she comes in the room. With her foot, she catches the door and shoves it closed. It's dark except for the hazy waning evening light coming through the window. I start to reach for her.

"Stop!" she gently commands me. "Stay right there."

I freeze.

She slowly begins to remove all her clothes.

"Florrie?" I turn my head toward her, the light from the reading lamp causing me to squint. She lowers her book and peers over her half glasses waiting for my question. "What's tenure?"

She smiles, takes her hand, and brushes my hair back. The book falls to the bed and flutters closed. "My god, what made you think of that?"

"Yesterday"—I reach up and grab her hand and hold it against my cheek—"you were talking about it with Jan and Lee."

"It's status assuring me a permanent position." She caresses me gently with her long fingers.

"I thought you had a permanent position?" I puzzle.

"Sometimes that takes years," she reflects. "Depends where you are."

"Funny." I drop her hand and snuggle close to her. "Never occurred to me that teachers would have to worry about permanent positions."

"Innocence," she whispers as she moves down in bed.

Jack and Eddie casually lean forward on the library table; each watches Mr. Putterman the school librarian walk toward the charge-out desk. I look at them and then turn and watch him too.

"Dean told me he's a faggot," Jack whispers to Eddie and me.
"How does he know?" I ask a bit too loudly.
"Shhhh" comes Mr. Putterman's hiss from across the room.

"'Course there's lots of things that never occurred to me
about teachers."

I brush my lips against her shoulder. She turns toward
me. I can feel the full length of her body. I reach around her
slowly, following the curve of her back, place my hand on
her buttocks, and pull her closer. I bury my face in her neck.
With my lips against her throat I ask, "What'll you do if you
don't get tenure?" I feel her stiffen and push back. She looks
down at me.

"Go to Israel," she says deliberately. "I've always wanted to
work on a kibbutz."

"Really?"

"Yes, really!" she gives a throaty laugh. "But in the moment
I want to make love." She takes my face in her hands and gives
me a deep kiss.

Driving up the hill to Brighton Park is like walking through
our relationship—circles and circles.

In the distance is her red Mustang, and she is sitting behind
the wheel. The steam from the exhaust dissipates in the cold
winter air. She looks up and sees me coming.

I pull my car up beside hers. I see her get out of her car.
I watch her walk around the front of mine. The collar on her
P-jacket pulled tight around her ears. Her ass is still cute.

The door opens, and those green eyes look at me and
tell me everything. Tears form in my eyes. She slides into the
front seat beside me. She reaches across and takes my face in
her hands.

"I'm sorry, Gail. Please don't cry," she whispers as she wipes
the tears from my face. Then those warm soft lips lightly brush
mine. "Good-bye."

She leaves.

I roll down the window and look at her just as she is getting into her car. "Why, Florrie?" I ask.

"'Cause."

CHAPTER 9

Vietnam

Circling several times, the plane begins a sharp decent into Ben Hoi Air Force Base, the lights of an occasional village dotting the darkness like jewels against black velvet.

With a loud bang, the tires of the aircraft hit the tarmac runway—we have arrived. Slowly, we come to a stop. The door to the aircraft opens.

A young specialist enters the aircraft. Standing before us he begins in a monotone:

"Good evening, ladies and gentlemen. Welcome to Ben Hoi Airfield." He takes his hand and wipes his forehead. "Before leaving the aircraft, please fill out these customs forms."

He begins a methodical walk down the aisle of the airplane, stopping at each row of seats to pass out both custom forms and pencils.

The silence is broken as he begins once again his monotone: "Once you leave the aircraft, go in single file and proceed directly to the terminal building."

The hot humid weather hits each of us like an old dishcloth as we exit the aircraft. The terminal building lurks as a dark figure before us.

"Short!"

"Next!"

"Sucker!"

"Fuckin' Lifer!"

A thunderous roar covers us as we enter the terminal building. To the left of us a mass of soldiers is waiting for us to exit the plane. Our entrance means their exit—the aircraft we just left is their ticket home.

"Christ, I made it," comes a shrill cry. "I really made it." It is followed by a whole string of obscenities about the parentage of Vietnam and where it belongs.

It is black, pitch black. The wire mesh covering on the windows of the bus doesn't help much either. Occasionally the moon peaks out behind eerie puffs of dark clouds, casting a foreboding glow on the surrounding countryside. It is then I can see the Jeep that leads the bus caravan. Two GIs stand behind a mounted .50 caliber machine gun in the back of the Jeep. I try to look off into the distance, but the darkness once again spills across my sight like flowing ink from an overturned inkbottle.

They told me I would be going to the old nurse's quarters instead of the WAC detachment. It means nothing; I have no sense of what should happen.

As the caravan begins its journey, I hear someone whisper that the wire mesh on the windows is to keep grenades from being tossed into the bus. I had thought it was to prevent passengers from sticking out their arms. As I look around, I see that each of us have unconsciously slouched into the seats, a pretense of sleep. The tops of heads are even with the bottom of the windows.

The brakes screech as we stop at a supply issue station. The driver calls out my name and tells me this where I get off. There is no baggage except my overnight case, so I easily exit from the bus.

The lamplights from carefully placed lanterns, like streetlights, give off a yellow glow, lighting the way on a web of wood sidewalks. I look around, unsettled by the strange silence. I walk straight toward the building in front of me. A weather worn sign, Incoming Personnel Report Here, hangs slight askew.

As I walk up the wooden sidewalk, I notice what looks like a duffel bag hanging from the tripod. Printed across the duffel bag in large black-stenciled letters—Potable Water. The hot blast of air splashes across my face; I scowl and continue walking. I plunk the twenty-five cents on the counter.

"Wow . . . real money. You must be new."

The young soldier shoves a set of sheets, a pillow, and an army green blanket over the counter toward me.

"How come they put you in the old nurses' quarters?" he asks.

"I have no idea," I say, hunching my shoulders.

"Ain't been anyone in them barracks for months," he proclaims. "You a medic?"

I shake my head.

"Just follow the sidewalk to the end." He points to my left.

As I walk down the wooden sidewalks toward the building, I hear the young soldier speaking on the telephone, the sound of his voice carried on the stifling night air. "Hey, we need a guard down at the old nurses' quarters."

The screen door creaks as I open it. At the end of a long hallway, with enclosed cubicles on each side, a television crackles, as the lines rotate constantly upward. I walk down the aisle peering into several cubicles. Each one has a bed and a nightstand. I turn around and see my footprints neatly outlined on the dusty floor. I return to the first cubicle.

I lay the army blanket on top of the bed and watch the faint cloud of dust rise and settle. I write my name on the top of the nightstand.

"Hey, is there anyone in there?"

I peek outside the cubicle door and turn my head toward the front door entrance.

A black silhouetted figure peers through the screen door.

"Yes." I swallow.

"Okay," the silhouette growls back. "I got picked for guard duty."

I look at the toilet stall entrance. I scratch my head and wonder who designed them. Twiggy?

If I use the toilet, there is no room to turn around. Guess I will have to back in, even then there is no room to reach up to pull my underpants down.

I turn my back to the stall door, reach up, and pull down my underpants to around my mid-calves. Taking small backward steps, I back into the toilet stall and sit on the toilet.

Looking around, I see the toilet paper holder high above on the right wall. I reach up and pull a sizable amount to use. I smile. I must first go out of the stall to use it.

No wonder they made new nurses' quarters.

He might be four or five, but I don't think much more. Barefoot, walking shorts and a ragged shirt. There is a stick in his hand. On his head, an army green baseball cap with captain's bars.

I watch him closely; he hasn't spotted me yet. He squats down, drops the stick, and carefully sifts dirt through his hands. I look at my watch; it's 6:30 in the morning. The air is filled with the smell of urine; reminds me of cat urine. The open sewer ditch is swelling with morning use. The mopeds haven't started their daily trips up and down the street. Across the way, a Vietnamese guard lifts his cap, looks at us, replaces it, and tries to go back to sleep. His weapon leans haphazardly against the tower wall.

The young boy sees me now. He drops the dirt and slaps his hands against his shorts as he stands and faces me. He swaggers in my direction.

Little bastard! Been living among the GIs. Cute little shit!

"Hey you, GI!" he calls out with confidence. I give no answer. "Me DiWee." He points to the insignia on his hat. I throw him a mock salute.

"You got cigarette," he asks, squinting.

"You're too young to smoke."

"Give me cigarette!" He grabs my arm with a tug. "Me DiWee."

"No!"

"Fuck you, GI." He grins as he throws me the bird.

He reaches in the pockets of his shorts, pulls out a Marlboro cigarette, places it in his mouth. He then takes a flip-top lighter and expertly cups his hand to protect the flame. With ease he inhales deeply and proceeds to blow smoke in my direction.

He winks and walks away.

The MP closes the lid to the briefcase. "Okay," he says.

I wave my hand as I walk out of the security check area. Automatically I reach up around my neck and place the security badge in my shirt. I look around to see what vehicles are parked in front. Sergeant Francis is loading a bag into a Jeep.

"Hey, Sergeant Francis," I call out. "You goin' over by the main gate?"

"Sure, hop in."

I quicken my pace, throw in my briefcase, and climb into the front seat. He jams the vehicle in reverse, shifts, and speeds down the road leaving a cloud of dust as we exit the Vietnamese compound. Turning right, he follows the triangle-shaped road around. In the middle of the triangle, there is high grass and a weathered billboard with the same old stylized picture of an Oriental woman smiling her eternal smile—it's been there from day one. Letters of a strange language telling those who can read it what product she wants you to buy.

As quickly as we started, Sergeant First Class Francis pulls off by the main gate. I grab my briefcase and jump out.

"Thanks." I hit the side of the Jeep. He spins away.

I walk to the gate guard. He waves me on through.

"Mind if I wait and catch a ride to the helicopter pad?"
He shakes his head.

Catching a ride, I walk into the operations desk and ask if they have any flights going to DiAn. They do. Twenty minutes.

The helicopter lifts and rises.

The pilot looks over and smiles at me. He can sense that I feel uneasy. I look down and see dozens of helicopters dotting the runway area, each prepared at a moment's notice for the short flight to Birmingham. The Alabama National Guard has been called to active duty to assist in controlling racial unrest. Claire, Gwen, and I came down to take a look at history being made, even though we'd been warned to stay away from this area. Some of the guys saw us, and here we are taking unauthorized joy rides.

"Ya ever seen a helicopter glide?" He laughs.

"Hell, I've never ridden in . . ." My stomach lurches as we drop like a stone. "Pleeeeeeeeeeeeeese," I gasp.

The aircraft continues to drop quickly, but a sense of control prevails.

"I've disconnected the main rotary blade from the motor shaft," he shouts. "That's what would happen in case of engine trouble.

I want to land. I couldn't give a shit about disconnected rotary blades. The aircraft thumps as the motor and shaft are once again united. He banks right and lands near the other helicopters.

Exiting the craft, one of the guys shouts that Claire and Gwen have gone to drink a beer. He points toward a large tent. In the background I hear a siren. A red light flashes near where he is pointing. MPs! Oh shit! I run and hide behind one of the helicopters. I peek around and see two MPs guiding Claire and Gwen to the waiting MP car. I watch the MP car turn toward us. I look around. I am alone. The guys have scattered to the winds. I can't stay here. I see a trashcan. If I hurry, I can make it there and hide. I scurry

toward the trashcan. Without looking, I jump inside, replacing the
lid. I can hear muffled voices. I pray no one looks inside the can.

The short ride to DiAn is ended. I jump from the aircraft
to gather some information for our unit history.

I stick out my thumb at a passing Jeep and run in the hot,
humid afternoon to catch my ride.

Whimpering with each step it takes, the puppy is supported
by three legs-the fourth hanging, a useless appendage, flopping
with each slight movement as it moves along the wall. It has
no fur. The ribs protrude, and the body is covered with open
sores. Maggots are writhing in rotting flesh.

"Stop!" I cry out to Lydia. She slams on the brakes of the
Jeep as she pulls off the road.

"What the hell?" She glances at me.

Pointing in the direction of the dog, I say, "Over there." I
jump out of the Jeep, waiting for traffic to go by.

The little one is still there. There is a slight movement. I see
a soldier come around the corner; the puppy directly before
him. The soldier steps back in disgust and then brings back his
leg and kicks. His booted foot connects with the side of the dog.
A yelp and I watch helplessly as the little one flies through the
air in a grotesque loop, falls, and lands in a cloud of dust.

"You FUCKING BASTARD," I yell at the soldier. He turns
to see me standing before him. I cock my leg and thrust the
toe of my boot at his crotch. Thud! My foot hits its target of
soft flesh.

"Arrrrgh," he screams as he bends over holding himself. I
turn to see Lydia holding the little one in a blanket.

A crowd has gathered. We run toward the Jeep. Lydia lays
the little pup on the floor. I glance over at the GI. He is still
cupping himself with his hands.

Dirt flies as we pull away from the side of the road onto
the main street.

I look back on the floor where the blanket lies. There is movement, a soft whimper, but I know there is no hope. Lydia reaches her hand out and touches my arm. She has seen the tears at the edge of my eyes.

We stop in front of the Vet's hooch. I scramble out and carefully pick up the little one. Lydia has already run ahead of me. Captain Williams opens the door, turns, and I automatically follow him.

Inside the exam room, I lay the pup on the table; and the blanket falls back. She lies there, her head rising slightly. The captain looks at me and shakes his head. Behind the Vet, a specialist prepares the syringe.

Holding her on the table, I cringe as the needle is inserted in the front leg. He pushes the plunger forward and almost instantly I feel the frail body go limp.

I put the blanket over her, the glassy eye still open. Lydia puts her arm around my shoulder as we walk out the door.

"Jesus, it was just a dog," I cry, "I didn't even know."

The Jeep leans to the right as we make our way toward the downtown section of Saigon. We pass by hundreds of mopeds overloaded with bananas and people. The stoplight provides a temporary diversion from all the noise.

The light is red at every corner. Pedestrians skittle across in hopes of missing the impending chaos. The motors are revved; the taxis wait impatiently. The light turns green, and all hell breaks lose. Lydia makes a jump start in the middle of the intersection. A horn blares followed by others. Z-i-i-i-p goes a blur of mopeds. A pedicab ducks in between her and the passing moped. The blast of an air horn on a 2 1/2 ton truck startles a water buffalo. A cart falls, fruits everywhere. Brakes, screech, wham! A mango flies through the air.

"Fuck you, GI" comes the perfect slang from the Vietnamese taxi driver followed by singsong verses that I am sure had something to do with our origins.

I peek from out of my hands which I had covered my eyes.

"Jesus, Lydia. This is pure suicide," I gasp.

She tosses her head back in laughter. "Survival of the fittest."

On the perimeter of some parcel of land, nestled at specific distances, a nest is built. Sometimes this nest contains stationary weapons and sometimes the nest is empty, filled only when the soldier brings his or her individual weapon with them.

In practice, the soldier fires on command in short, sharp bursts of three rounds, the rhythm unbroken as the select switch on the side of the M16 is placed on "semiautomatic." In reality, you hope it's a dream. There are usually two soldiers per nest; and the weapon is pointed forward, moved from side to side in slow to medium pace at a forty-five-degree frontal area with intersecting areas from each weapon. This assures that maximum firing power is utilized using a minimum of weapons. This is called "establishing fields of fire."

They remind me of drive-in theater screens—miniature, of course. They look so nonviolent. On one side is printed FRONT TOWARD ENEMY. They have a little stand to set them on. At the top are two terminals. Screw-type terminals.

The guys carefully place the "little screens" on the outside perimeter of the compound. Setting them at the appropriate distance, making sure that the fields of fire intersect. The wires are carefully attached to each terminal and buried as they run along the ground. Finally, after all the mines are laid, all wires buried, the antipersonnel mines are connected to the detonating device.

Lydia and I have been sitting here for the last half hour watching this ritual. The guys are finished and return to our area.

"Ya'll want a beer?" Randy asks.

We both shake our heads.

"I need to get these papers back to personnel," proclaims Lydia. "Come on, Randy, sign these things." He walks toward her. Taking the pen out of his fatigue shirt pocket, he quickly scribbles his name.

Lydia takes the papers and puts them in her briefcase. We head out for the Jeep. I hesitate, slowly turn around, and look out once more just beyond where the mines have been laid. I sigh as I climb into the Jeep.

We three, Norma, Lydia and I, walk down the noisy street, the mopeds zipping by. Our nostrils flare as we walk by a pile of open garbage. Big black swarms of flies rise and fall around the heap.

Coming toward us is a young soldier, twirling his body round and round, his eyes scanning all that surrounds him. His back is to us; and as he spins around, he stops dead in his tracks. He sees us and freezes.

We look at each other and then at him.

"Stop!" he yells. We are so startled we do just that. "Don't move . . . please," he continues.

"Round eyes . . . my god round eyes," he repeats continually.

The young Vietnamese woman follows Norma and me to the toilet. She is closer to Norma than to me. Her tight blue dress moves like natural skin with each step she takes. Her eyes are exaggerated with black liner. Her jet-black hair is pulled tightly back, held with a comb; and the ponytail falls to just below her buttocks. The front of her dress dips into a deep V-shape. The fleshy mounds of her breasts are pinched together to give her the appearance of ample breasts.

I open the door to the toilet and quickly move to an unoccupied stall.

"God damn it," I hear Norma grumble. "I don't need any help!"

"What's up, Norma?" I ask from where I sit.

"Gail," she exclaims, "this woman is trying to come in the stall with me."

I chuckle . . . .

"It's not funny, Gail." I hear scuffling and unintelligible words

"You need help?" I ask. "Hold on, I'm coming." I pull my fatigue pants up and open the stall door with my butt as I finish buckling my belt.

The woman is standing outside the stall door where Norma has entered, waiting. She puts her hands on her hips, smiles, and walks toward me.

"Hey you, GI." She winks at me.

"Me Co . . . woman," I say. "Me no GI."

"Same, same." She smiles. Her teeth are beautiful. She doesn't have that lychee nut red/black stain on her teeth. "You give me money, I show you good time."

She runs her fingers up and down my forearm, stopping momentarily to pull the hair on my arm.

I take her hand and gently move it away from my arm. "No want good time."

"Why you here if you no want good time?" she asks. I shrug my shoulders.

"GIs always want good time." She gives me a blank look. "You crazy GI." She turns and walks out the door.

"She gone?" calls out Norma.

"Yeah."

Norma comes out of the stall. "Wow! That was weird." She walks to the sink and washes her hands.

I turn and twist the water on. "Survival," I say as I shake the water from my hands.

We walk back out into the main bar room. Off in the corner I see the blue silk skin standing next to a GI. His hands cover her tiny ass as he rubs her in a circular motion. The tight dress creeps up higher.

"Come on, Norma." I turn toward her. "Let's get the hell out of here."

A gurgling sound followed by a shallow grunt comes from behind me. Both Lydia and I turn in unison.

The child that is before us holds up a small tin cup with two fleshy growths from an almost perfectly formed arm. He looks and moves like a caterpillar, only his legs are two platforms with wheels. The fleshy mass of hair and skin forms an enormous tumor extending from the top of his head all along the right side of his face and entire body. If there is an arm, it is not discernible at first glance. His face is terribly distorted, with the right eye located almost where his chin would end. It is nonfunctional, appearing to be only the white eyeball. His nose and mouth are one form, giving him the look of an adult dog.

"Oh Jesus." Lydia grabs her mouth and closes her eyes. Verbalizing the revulsion we both feel.

My first reaction is to grab Lydia and walk away as fast as we can. He moves closer to us by putting the tin cup on the edge of his platform and with his good arm, pulls himself along the sidewalk. The massive tumor in snakelike fashion follows him, stretching and gliding behind him. A seasoned beggar, he is not about to let us go away.

We look at each other and quietly reach in our fatigue pockets, take out one hundred piaster, and carefully place them in his extended tin cup.

He puts the cup down once again. He bows his head, the movement causing a ripple to travel down the growth to the very end on the second platform where it stops in a bubble like form.

We politely turn away and continue to walk. The slide—scrape slide—scrape of his movement seems louder the farther away we go.

It's a gray day. Big puffs of clouds darken the sky. But it's hot. Payday is a day to wait in line.

The bank. I have seen nothing like it. There is a large building with a tarmac surface surrounding it. Fifty or more windows are wrapped around the structure, and all fifty-some windows will open at once. Lines began forming hours before opening time. Many are grunts in from the bush; the mud and filth still caked to their boots and uniforms. Some wear bush hats, others wear camouflage head bands. M16 rifles are slung over the shoulder with the barrels pointing down. Clip removed. Steel pots, some on their heads, with the familiar "peace" symbol crudely drawn. Some wear sleeves rolled up, some have the sleeves cut off, and some wear no shirts. Beside them the Saigon Warrior with freshly polished boots, clean uniform, and a close shave.

Scattered throughout the crowd, a rhythmic flow can be seen and heard. The familiar "Dap." It is as varied as the men who perform them. An elaborate hand jive ritual with a partner, simple and complicated, movements lasting from a few minutes to more than an hour.

Shortly before opening time, the area is a mass of green and black—a collage of earth tones. Lines have haphazardly formed, one hundred people deep. Some are standing, some lying flat deep in sleep, others pacing back and forth.

The windows open like the gates at a horse race. Transactions begin. At first everyone waits with controlled patience. As the day wears on, nerves begin to frazzle, tempers begin to show. Bank clerks occasionally look out to see a never-ending line, then bow their head, dreading if nature calls.

The first window closes with a quick, surprising movement. No one expects it. The clerks have long ago learned that they should give no warning. The metal bars and wood shutters drop like a guillotine simultaneously.

The grunt jumps forward, pounding on the shutters and shaking the steel bars.

"Ya fucker!" he shouts as he slaps the shuttered window. "Ya Goddamn motherfucker."

Quietly a hand without a body appears in the window, slips a lettered sign: *This window will reopen at 1300.*

Once again the line settles down. Some take their chances at another line; most just wait.

Jo and Lydia are sitting on the bed. I am sitting on the chair by the dresser, and Lucky is lying flat on the floor. In the center of the unlikely circle is a pile of cards.

"Four spades," says Jo.

I pass.

There's a flash of light. Blast! In slow motion, glass breaks and falls. No movement. Lydia and Jo throw themselves on the floor. The chair falls over as I dive for the bottom. Flash of light. Blast! Crack! There is a screen of dust as the corner of the room collapses. The wall teeters back and forth. It won't sustain another blast.

"Let's get the fuck out of here," someone hollers.

We all scramble toward the door—wide open, torn from the hinges. The hallways to the hotel are empty. We make our way toward the stairways. In the background sirens wail to almost a scream. There's smoke everywhere and the bright orange color of fire. We cannot go any farther. Our hope lies toward the other stairwell. The heat is intense; the smoke thick as the color black.

"Crawl, you guys! Get on the Goddamn floor."

Lydia is leading; we make our way along the wall of the hallway, past Jo's room toward the other stairwell.

"Hurry, Jesus fucking hurry," yells Jo. "The heat is biting my butt."

There is a stairwell door. Lydia pushes on it. It is locked. We all try. Wait. No. It's not locked. Something is in front blocking it from opening. We push our way through. A Vietnamese woman lies slumped near the door. Is she dead or hurt? We hesitate. We all know that we can't leave her here. She moans. Lydia and I take her arms. The stairwell is clear. No smoke here. We struggle with the woman as we try quickly but gently to help her walk down the stairs.

We burst out into the lobby of the hotel. People are scurrying everywhere. The lobby is filled with smoke. Everyone is trying to push through the doors.

We lay the woman down. Jo and Lucky take her between the two of them, one arm on Jo the other on Lucky. Lydia and I help them toward the front door. Shoved and bumped, we break to the outside, each of us gasping for fresh air. A medic takes the woman from our hands.

"Are any of you hurt?" he asks. No one answers.

"Come on! We got to get the hell out," whispers Lydia.

We look for a ride.

Lydia leans over the edge of the roof scanning the skyline; she points in the direction of the street below. I follow the direction of her outstretched arm.

The bicycle rider carries bananas in a small bunch. All but one is tucked under his arm. Balancing with ease, pedaling with little effort, his hand holds the fruit; and he quickly peels the outer shell and stuffs the ripe banana in his mouth. With a graceful flick of his hand, the banana peel loops through the air and over the fence near the guard watchtower.

There is instantaneous movement from the guard tower. Lydia and I watch as the guard brings the weapon to his shoulder. Crack! It is like the sound of whip on a cold crisp morning. Time slows as the face of the bicycle rider looms before us in unreal dimensions. The eyes wide, his mouth opens without sounds, and a trickle of blood spills over the edge.

The rider loops backward off the bicycle, bounces, and skids into the ditch. The bicycle wobbles in forward movement then crashes in a heap.

Lydia and I turn to each other. Nausea makes us gag momentarily. Without words we run to the stairwell, scramble down the stairs past the dayroom, and burst outside to the front of our hotel quarters. We stop. A Vietnamese policeman takes the arms of the bicycle rider and slowly drags him toward a waiting taxicab. A sandal falls away from the dragging foot. The rider's head hangs backward. His face is partially missing. Off by the ditch, another policeman is kicking dirt over the fresh pool of blood.

Lydia grabs my arm, and her fingers dig into my flesh.

The cabdriver opens the door to the backseat of the vehicle. Together he and the policeman stuff the body into the car.

The cab moves away. The policemen mount the moped and start to drive away, hesitate, and then one of them reaches down and snatches up the lost sandal.

It is raining hard. Monsoon season. Poor Carolyn, one of the encryption specialists at work, has fallen three times. The last time I literally "dived" under the knee-high water to pull her up. What does she do but laugh—a happy drunk however.

Carolyn keeps to herself. The three of us have decided that she needed to let her hair down. All dressed up in fatigues—what else—we made our way to the Headquarters Area Command Club dragging Carolyn behind. She sputterd and offered her usual resistance, but we decided that no was an unacceptable answer.

After an institutional steak, we watched the show. Tonight the big feature was a band from Australia. The guys loved it. The "round eyes" drove them crazy. Terry, our one air force buddy, Lydia and I silently conspired to get Carolyn drunk. We kept pouring Mateus wine in her glass. Our conspiracy was successful; Carolyn is now obnoxious and happy—and drunk.

It takes the three of us to get her on the bed. We take off to Terry's room to spend the rest of the evening playing cards. It's rummy—our spades partner is lying in a drunken stupor.

It's time to check on Carolyn.

I open the door ever so slightly. I walk into her room. Carolyn has been up. She is laying on her back, completely naked, her legs draped over the end of the bed. Around her neck, the one thing none of us ever take off, the security badge. She is snoring. I cover her with the bed sheet. Carolyn is shy. She'll be embarrassed if she realized I saw her this way. I would too, and I am now; and she is not even awake.

I walk out of the room and silently close the door. Taking the steps two at a time, I knock on Terry's door. Lydia and Terry are sitting waiting for me to return to finish our game of rummy.

"Well?" Lydia asks.

I smile. "She's asleep."

The chopper rises and banks sharply to the right then climbs higher. The effect is not unlike retracting a telescopic lens on a camera to get a wide-angle view. Than San Nhut Airfield shrinks and the triangle of the roads around the area is more pronounced as we rise even higher. Our destination, a little more than an hour to reach, is a small village near the Parrot's Beak on the Cambodian border.

Every since the Vietcong had started their offensive through the northern provinces of Cambodia, more and more refugees had begun their desperate flight into Vietnam. Many mothers abandoned children at orphanages or churches, in hopes that they would be given the care the parents felt they could not provide. These mothers realized that it was certain death for their young if they carried them along. Our unit had hoped to transfer at least twenty of the babies to the orphanage we support in Cholon outside of Saigon. It was better equipped to handle the extra influx of children. Intelligence had informed us that the North Vietnamese Army had intended to enter Vietnam through the Parrot's Beak. The small village was the focal point of that insertion.

Lydia and I volunteered to help with the transfer of children. We sat quietly listening to the ever-present whamp!

Whamp! of the rotary blades. We wouldn't be able get all of the babies in the chopper; but at the briefing, we were informed that it would be several weeks before the NVA would reach the border. We could still make another pick up before it became critical.

Lydia looks out of the aircraft, taking in the breathtaking scenery of lush green jungle, interspersed with rice paddies and the mirror like reflections of light of the still water below. The spider web of small rivers and creeks peeks out almost as if waiting for its next victim. It was deceiving, this scene from above. Below lurked many dangers. The false cloak of serenity covered those horrors.

"Are you okay?" She smiles, gently curving the corner of her lip. The dimple, like a stone thrown into water, ripples and is suspended for a moment then dissipates.

"Ya," I sighed, "just thinking about things."

"Me too."

Silence.

"We're almost there!" Warrant Officer Nation shouts over the loud whamp whamp of the helicopter. "There." He points to an old rice field next to a dense overgrowth of foliage.

"Move quickly! Good luck!" He gives us the thumbs up.

Once again the chopper banks left and then right as we descend toward our destination. We see, in the distance, a fury of activity near the old rice paddy. It is the sisters with our precious cargo. The debris flies in small whirlwinds, and the habits of the nuns strain against their thin bodies as our chopper hovers above the ground. Lydia jumps the short distance to the ground. I follow right on her heels as we begin to run toward our waiting party.

Kaa-thump! Terrified, we see in slow motion impending doom, unfolding before us. I leap forward, thrusting my entire weight to bring both Lydia and myself to the soggy earth. A sharp pain shoots through my left arm. Dirt and clumps of earth fall around us like a hailstorm. The noise is deafening and consuming. Then total silence.

Behind me I hear the chopper motors revving faster.

"Westbrook!" comes the desperate cry, "It's Charlie! Get the hell out! I'll be back." With that he was gone, followed by another ka-thump! The explosion of dirt and debris is several yards on the other side where the helicopter had been.

Oh shit! I might die, but there is nothing left to do but crawl. Concentrate on the kids. I think out here you are a sitting duck. I can't hear, the blast keeps repeating, repeating.

Where the fuck is Lydia? The tall grass parts slowly as I crawl forward. There is no pain in my arm. Funny, I thought there would be more pain. Crawling like this is like driving in a dense fog, stomach muscles tight, mouth dry like cotton— scared to death. I glance to my right where Lydia is crawling, elbow, knee alternating. This damn steel pot is heavy. Jesus, what will I do if the next time the grass parts I'm looking down the barrel of an AK47? I don't even know what the hell they look like.

I gotta look. Gotta get our bearings, we could go on forever. I reach back and touch Lydia's arm.

"Lydia, I gotta look where we are." I can't think straight. "Gotta find out if we are crawling in the right direction."

She makes no sound; her dark eyes reflect her understanding.

I straighten my legs. I put my hands on the ground near my upper chest, I raise myself on all fours. Waiting to see how long I'm going to live.

My eyes dart back and forth. There within spitting distance of Lydia and me—oh God—Little legs twisted and torn from its torso. Hanging by a thread, there is no face, just raw meat. I throw myself flat; I hear a gagging sound. It's me. I'm puking right there on the ground. My fingers grasp the earth and grass and mud. I try to scream. My mouth opens, but no sound comes out.

Lydia is beside me. She raises herself to her knees. I reach to grab her and whisper.

"Don't, Lydia, Jesus fucking Christ don't!"

She twists to her right, and I see her shoulders lurch forward as she heaves and vomits.

One sister lies in a broken heap face down, a jagged hole torn through flesh and spine. Underneath, a small foot protrudes out from her chest. Movement!

"Look!" Lydia shouts pointing to the moving foot. "There's a baby under her!" She pushes the body of the sister away. Gasping for air with a resounding protest, the small baby cries out.

In the background, we hear the b-d-d-d-t, the short bursts of a machine gun, and the familiar whamp! whamp! of the chopper blades. I look up toward the sound and see Mr. Nation making circles around the area, while Specialist Bluewater fires with deadly accuracy at our unseen attackers. The chopper is heading back toward us.

Lydia and I frantically continue to find the survivors. Five sisters lie dead with ten of the babies among them. The other sisters help us collect the remaining children. There are eight in all, two badly wounded. The chopper hovers close by us, barely skimming the earth. Specialist Bluewater jumps from the chopper and runs toward us.

"Hurry!" he shouts, "A whole fuckin NVA Battalion is coming!" Running toward one of the sisters, he grabs a wounded baby and runs for the chopper.

One by one, we rush to load our cargo. Everyone is on. Lydia puts her foot on the skid as Specialist Bluewater grabs her hand.

The telescopic illusion repeats as the chopper rises and heads toward the Third Field Hospital.

I get out of the Jeep. Before me is a sea of kids—Cambodian. In the short distance, squatting in front of a large tin building with a gaping hole for a door, are the adults—only a handful. They watch me with gathering suspicion and curiosity.

Sergeant Major told me I would be the first white woman they had ever seen.

I turn around to help unload the bags of rice, but I am unable to move my arms. The hair on my arm fascinates the kids. They pull it to see if it is real.

The Cambodian women come forward and quietly take the rice.

I am walking toward the large reservoir. I look at the water. There are enormous carp swimming and writhing in the murky liquid. I wonder why they are so large. There is barely enough food for all these refugees, let alone the fish.

Over the reservoir is a wooden house. I watch as a one-legged old man hobbles to enter the building. A moment later, from under the structure, a small mass drops. The carp surge and twist causing the water to boil angrily. They are fighting over the piece of waste deposited by the old man.

The long rows of wooden tables spread out over the room. The child I hold in my arms fidgets in his sleep, but for the most part, rests his cheek against my fatigue shirt.

I watch Lydia walk across the great hall from the rice pots to where a small girl is sitting, her dark eyes level with the top of the table. She struggles to scoop rice from a small bowl that she holds with a well-healed stump. Most of the rice falls, and the bowl rocks back and forth, threatening to roll away.

Lydia increases her stride. Her long legs make it look easy. With a quick step she bends forward as the bowl falls. She catches it and places it back on the table.

Lydia straddles the bench, sits down, and places the child upon her knee. With Lydia holding the bowl, the child begins to eat. Each time the child's mouth opens Lydia's mouth opens.

The bowl of rice finished, Lydia holds a glass of milk. The child drinks quickly. She pulls away and grins, the white half circle of milk painting a smile upon her face. She wiggles and squirms pushing herself away from Lydia and runs toward the groups of kids playing with a ball. Laughter fills the air.

Dark black eyes sparkle, and her smile exposes brilliant white teeth. She is part Vietnamese, part American; she wears a badly fitting dress with a hundred patches and stands in bare feet.

She shyly makes her way behind the other children, paper plate in hand. She drops her eyes when I look in her direction. The smile stays there on her face as if she sees some unknown secret lying upon the ground.

The children come forward and bravely hold their plates as high as their arms will allow, as I carefully place the food on them. They quietly pass on to the next station.

She is next. She stands in front of me and lifts up her plate. It's not very high. Then I see the scar tissue. It won't allow her to stretch her arm. Her arm is a mass of angry red welts, and her burned hand has healed in a web shape. I bend down and dish out the food. She looks at me, and that smile spreads across her face like rain drops in a pond. She brings the plate to waist level, and I wait for her to move on, but she hesitates. Then carefully, with a nod, she bows gently toward me in a gesture of thanks.

The children move through the line. We fill our plates and join them. My eyes search for her, and I find her, with another little girl. I walk toward her, pointing to myself, then to the ground beside her.

She nods. I sit down. They both giggle and then we three quietly begin to eat.

I can see she is waiting for me to finish. When I do, I stand. She timidly takes my paper plate and dashes off to find a trashcan.

As quickly as she left, she returns, touches my arm, and looks at me. With her webbed hand, she beckons me to follow her. We walk to the side of the building. A trestle of tropical flowers covers the wall. She points high in the corner. My eyes search in the direction she is pointing. Hanging delicately above us on a long thin thread is an enormous spider swaying back and forth in the gentle breeze. Above the spider is a magnificent web in beautiful geometric designs.

The spider suddenly scrambles up the thread and across the web in a dark corner. She watches and laughs. Then as I am about to walk away, she turns and hugs me. With my arm resting on her shoulder, we return to the others.

We are off to Thailand.

The sun bakes.

A single bead of sweat forms on my forehead and follows an irregular path down the side of my face. Almost everyone stands around, while Lydia and I sit on our suitcases. There is no shade.

It feels funny being in "civvies." The soft material of my white blouse feels foreign, out of place here in this country. I glance quickly in Lydia's direction; she scans the horizon as if expecting a sudden change in the weather.

A blackboard hanging slightly askew bears a message hastily printed with damp chalk that the R&R flight to Bangkok had been delayed for one hour.

Stretching, I stand, trying to cover up my response to look once again at Lydia. I carelessly let my eyes follow the lines of her body. I had never seen her in "civvies," and the skirt allows me to glance at the strong shape of her long legs.

Our eyes meet, she smiles; and the dimple captures me, brings me back.

"I hope we have a nice room," she sighs.

"Me too." I wipe the sweat off my face. "'Course most anything will be nicer than the Medford."

She nods in agreement.

The steps creak and groan as each of us moves down the exit ladder of the airplane to the tarmac below. It smells slightly sweeter here. It still feels hurried, a frantic electric rush to get moving.

Lydia turns and looks at me smiles and winks. I feel the warmth rise, like the shadowy, wavy lines that rise from a heat mirage.

We follow all the men walking toward a huge Quonset hut like a hanger. The movements into the dark building from the bright outside light make me feel uneasy, not knowing what is on the other side. I hear voices; and as my eyes adjust to the darker light inside, I see a large group of women lined up against the wall. I look to see that Lydia has wrinkled her forehead and wonders as I do.

"I want her man and her too," a clean-shaven young man exclaims.

"Oh my god, I think I am in love," sighs another.

As I come closer I see that each young woman, most of them Thai I guess, have some sort of sign hanging from their neck.

"Did you read that?" whispers Lydia.

I shake my head. "No, what is it?"

"Health certificates."

It glistens, and seems to be freer, but the sounds and the smell appear the same. Have we circled and come back to Vietnam and I think I am in Bangkok?

As we process through the R&R Station, I feel the vigilance leave, a kind of relaxed awareness. We will head toward the International Hotel right in the center of the city. It is one of the best they advertise. Small beads of sweat trickle down the side of my face as I push the paper money toward the R&R center clerk. The hotel must be prepaid.

The cab waits. Black smoke surrounds the little car as we hurriedly push in our luggage. I give him a piece of paper with the address of the hotel.

The noisy mopeds zip past us as we jerk to a start. I can see the palm trees swaying in the slight tropical breeze. Vendors with bananas and candy like dog flesh wave their wares at the GIs pouring out of the building on their way to a week of denial or forgetting or pocketed fear.

Dodging in and out, sliding from side to side, screeching to an incomplete stop, the little cab finds the end of our seemingly never-ending puzzle. It stops before a paradise—the International Hotel. I don't think it's the right place. Lydia grabs my arm.

"We're here!"

The hotel bellhop carries our luggage to the room. The plush carpet gives as we walk into the room, all done in greens, grays, and white. I hand him his tip.

"Hey, wait a minute!" Lydia shouts from the bedroom.

"I thought we had two double beds?"

I look in the bedroom. The circular bed occupies the majority of the room. It would take a three-day pass just to get from one side to the other.

"You wanna change?" I ask.

She glances away from me, "No, not really . . ." The words drop to a whisper.

I look away, trying to muffle the sound of my heart.

I look away. Looking at her would give me away stupefy me. I hear her footsteps as she nears the pool; she speaks to me. "Where are *you*?" She asks, emphasizing the word you.

I turn my head and lock my gaze in her eyes. I feel a quick sudden intake of breath. I feel the heat creep toward my face, and I see the rise of her breasts. I know I am getting shorter as my ankles turn to butter in the hot Thailand sun.

She jumps into the pool. I feel relieved that the water has hidden the source of my uncomfortable moment.

The bartender, a small man, and well-tanned, half-walks, half-swims behind the glass stone bar located in the swimming pool. I walk down the steps toward the bar, knowing I can look at Lydia swimming laps in the main pool.

I order a Coke with lime.

Her stroke in the water is rough and uneven. It makes it easy to follow her wherever she is. Funny, I thought she might cut the water with easy silent strokes.

She stops, treads water, and waves to me. I wave back, and then motion her to come to the bar. She starts to swim toward me.

The coolness of the room circles us. Makes goose bumps form up and down my arm. Outside, a gentle rain leaves tiny drops to form on the window, then snake their way to the bottom, distorting the lights of the night Bangkok sky—crystals flashing and blinking.

I plop down in the easy chair, exhausted from the day's activities, full from the dinner we just ate. I lean back and close my eyes.

I startle, my eyes darting from corner to corner of the room. Hazy, foggy recollection and like a veil of lace that lifts I realize where I am. I have no idea how long I have been here. The room is partially dark; I do not see Lydia. She has gone to bed.

I walk toward the bedroom. The dim lights of the night lamp give off a warm glow. Lydia stands before the dressing room mirror. Just as I approach the door, the towel that she has around her falls in a gentle heap on the rug. For an instant, before I look away, too embarrassed to say anything, I see the supple breast and the strong body bathed in the exotic shadow of light. I quickly turn and walk from the bedroom, certain that she heard me or at least she has heard the thundering pounding of my heart.

"Lydia," I call, half-swallowing, "are you in bed?'

"Not quite," she answers back, "just finished my shower." The towel is fully in place as I reenter the room.

Relieved that she did not know I had been there earlier, I make toward the shower.

As I climb in bed, I hear the gentle breathing of Lydia. Is she asleep? I lay there, eyes like an owl peering into the night, wanting her to be awake.

Early morning comes quickly. The light through the rain-streaked window is like a prism, casting bent rays of color over the room. Lydia is still sleeping, and I lie here watching the colors play upon her skin. Trying hard not to touch her, not to wake her.

The tour guide tries desperately to get our attention; everyone is talking in quick short bursts. Several of the guys are draped over their seats, heads back, mouths wide open, while their selected escorts talk in the singsong Thai language. A young woman has opened the flashy shirt of one young man and rubs the hairy chest in wide circles, sometimes combing the dark curly hair with long fingernails. He snores loudly.

"Test, test . . . hello," intones the tour guide. The microphone crackles intermittently. She once again brings the microphone close to her mouth.

"Do hear me?" She looks at Lydia and me. We nod. "You know what bananas are good for?" We both shrug our shoulders and shake our heads.

"Tourists and monkeys!" She replies her eyes sparkle as she gives us a mischievous grin. We both stop peeling the bananas we carry. We laugh.

The moss hangs from the trees. The sunlight peeping over the top of the dense forest brings eerie shadows along the riverbank. Our boat glides silently through the still water. Shack after shack passes by, some alive with people greeting the new day, some quiet like the river that runs by.

Lydia is slightly scrunched in the seat beside me. Her head is resting in her hand, her elbow on the side of the boat. I watch her as she fights to stay awake. Her dark eyes are half-covered by drooping eyelids. Long, curly eyelashes bounce each time she tries to open her eyes. Her unsmiling face hides her dimples. Her naturally pink full lips are slightly parted showing a hint of her wonderful white teeth. The breeze gently stirs her dark auburn hair, closely cut and styled. The large sweeping curl in front threatens to fall from its place.

She is sound asleep. She no longer fights the inevitable. I fight the urge to collect her to my shoulder. Her long legs stretch out before her. I watch the rise and fall of her breasts against her blouse as she breathes.

I look away and realize that the river is widening, and the forest has faded away. The shacks are no longer visible along the edge. The sun slowly makes its way higher in the sky. The view is spectacular. I reluctantly touch Lydia's arm. She would want to see this.

As I touch her, she stirs and slowly opens her eyes. She focuses and locks them on me. I smile and point in the direction of the riverbank.

The sunlight reflected off the multicolored tiles of the temples gives the Bangkok skyline a fantastic jeweled look.

Our time is fast coming to an end. Tomorrow we will return to Vietnam. As we enter our room, a bottle of cheap wine had been placed on the table, courtesy of the management for all parting guests. Neither Lydia nor I wanted to try it. The icy water was quickly becoming room temperature.

"I think I will read awhile," I lie as I turn and look at Lydia.

"Okay." She turns and walks toward the bedroom.

I curse myself for being such a fool. I walk to the patio. Standing in the darkness, I look over the garden. Black shadows mark where large trees stand. The lights cast a faint glow on the path across the grounds. The muffled sounds of passing mopeds and cars engulf me, help me think of other things.

"Gail" comes the sound, as if a feather on the wind. I squint and turn my head slightly to see if the sound will come again, not believing I had heard anything. Movement. It is Lydia. She touches my cheek with her hand.

"Am I wrong?" she whispers.

"No," I answer.

"Are you cold?" she whispers as her lips touch my ear. I feel the words more than hear them.

"No."

"Shhhh." She places my head on her breast.

Gently my hand caresses her back and then touches the soft skin of her side. She arches her back and thrusts her breast to my waiting lips. This is a tender beautiful woman.

Lydia pulls my robe from my shoulders and with her hands pushes it down and then the robe and her hand become one, caressing my skin as they slowly slide.

There is nothing between us, as we discover each other there on the rug of that room in Bangkok. Touching, feeling, caressing, and rising to an ecstasy that had lain dormant for so long. Feelings long put aside. It would never be the same, and we both knew we never wanted it to be the same.

We lie together in the bed, holding on as if tomorrow must never come, desperately savoring our moment together.

I rise upon my elbow, our legs intertwined, my other hand brushing over the soft skin of her cheek. "I'm glad you came to me like that," I clear my throat. "I was so scared I would scare you away if I let you know how I felt."

"I have known from the moment we picked up those kids, but I had no idea how to tell you." She moves slightly toward me. "When I saw you standing there in the dark, it was almost as if you had called to me."

We kiss, and it begins all over again. Way into the light of the early morning I am envious that the rays of the sun can touch the day the way I want to touch Lydia, forever, quietly, all at once and with such splendor.

We are back in Vietnam; the smell of used ammunition shells permeates the air. Things are not the same; it has all changed. I look at her differently now.

"Do you suppose"—she fingers the dog tag chain around her neck—"what's between us would have happened if we hadn't gone to pick up those kids?"

Careful, Gail. Sitting on the floor, I look at her, she's testing. I grab the shoe brush from the desk and begin a wide back and forth stroke on my dusty boots.

"I don't know"—pausing for just a second—"about you. I liked you from the beginning."

She jumps up from the chair. "I'm going up to the roof." She opens the screen door to my room and disappears as quickly as her question was asked.

I lay the shoe brush back on the desk. Maybe she wants to be alone. No, she must want to talk. Oh, hell, I'm going up there. If she wanted to be alone, she wouldn't have told me where she was going.

I walk up the short flight of stairs to the roof. I turn the corner. I can see her holding on to the railing near the makeshift movie screen. The skyline of Saigon dwarfs her as she leans forward with her face in her hands and her elbows resting on the railing. I stop and watch her, trying to decide if I should go farther. She stands up, looks back at me; she smiles.

"Well"—she looks off into the distance—"are you just going to stand there?" I walk toward her, and both of us look out over the city.

I pull out a cigarette, giving it to her, and then take one myself. Lighting hers then mine, we stand seemingly waiting for the other to say something.

"I feel so right with you," she blurts out. "But . . ." She turns around leaning her butt against the railing and folding her arms against her chest, the cigarette grasped between her fingers.

I swallow, "But what?" I try not to flinch. A single bead of sweat runs down the small of my back.

"I can't help but think where it puts me . . . us." She looks at me.

"I don't understand," I scowl. I throw the cigarette down and grind it out with my foot.

"Jesus, Gail!" She takes a drag off her cigarette, "It puts us outside the norm!"

"What norm?" I challenge.

"The . . . the sexual norm," she drops the last words off to a whisper.

"Sexual norm!" Easy, Gail, I scold myself. I take a deep breath and let it out slowly. "Are you sorry?" I tense, waiting for the blow of her words.

"That's just it," she flips her cigarette out over the edge. "I keep thinking I should be sorry . . . but I'm not."

The sky behind us far off to the west begins to boil as the rain clouds gather momentum. The thunder rolls and growls. We watch several Vietnamese women whittle away with short-handled shovels at a huge pile of dirt as a group of men sit watching them. The men play some sort of game. The women carefully fill a wheelbarrow with dirt; once filled, it is rolled off by a wisp of a woman, almost childlike, into a disappearing street. I wonder if Lydia is also marveling how this tiny woman has found the strength.

She shakes her head. "Amazing, isn't it?"

I nod mine.

"You know," she begins again, "I know there are gay women in the military." She takes a deep breath and rubs her arms up and down. "Live and let live. They didn't bother me, and I wasn't interested." She reaches for another cigarette and lights it, taking a long drag. "Curious maybe."

"This is hard for you." I smile at her. "I want to hold you . . . you know that?"

"That's why I wanted to talk up here." She walks over and sits on one of the sand bags. "I don't function rationally when you hold me. Here!"—she puts her fist over her heart, hitting her chest—"it feels so normal . . . so right." She puts her fist on her head, knocking. "Here, I have learned that it is wrong."

I watch her as she throws herself against the wall of sandbags.

"There's that word again." I say.

"What word?" she puzzles.

"Normal."

"Oh . . ." She closes her eyes. "Don't tell me you think that what we do is normal?"

"Different . . . just different, Lydia." I drum my fingers along the railing. "But I sure as hell don't consider it abnormal."

"I'm so fucking confused, Gail." She pounds the sandbag with her fist. "I love you, but I can't handle being called a l . . . l . . . lesb—"

"Whoa!" I put up my hands. "No one said you had to label yourself!"

Whamp! Whamp! Whamp! The sound growing louder as we look and see a dust-off helicopter making its way to the Third Field Hospital. The flight path takes the aircraft directly over our building. She stands up, and we go to the opposite side and watch it as it lands. The hospital personnel, like ants, run with haste toward them as the helicopter touches down on the pad. They grab a stretcher and rush with orchestrated ease back toward the emergency room area. A medic hustles beside them holding an IV over his head.

"Lydia," I touch her cheek, then quickly draw my hand away. "For what it's worth, I never liked that label anyway."

A loud deafening roar and then a big splash of water hit us both. The sky begins to open up and instantly we are drenched. We run to the stairwell and rush inside. We are both laughing.

Her laughter drops away. "Gail," she looks at me, the rainwater dripping from her hair, running down her face, "do you have time . . . time to wait while I wrestle with this thing?"

"Yeah." I wipe the water from her nose. "Forever," I whisper.

We turn and walk down the stairs.

"Did you read this?" she asks, peering over the newspaper and looking at me.

"Which one?" I ask.

"The soldier selling classified material to the Russians."

I shake my head. "Naw. I just looked at the headlines."

"Says they threatened him with snapshots of him and some woman having sex."

"It had to be more than that." I look at her with doubt.

"Why?" She puts the paper down and peers at me. "What would you do if they showed you pictures of you and me?"

"Look at them," I chuckle and wink at her.

"No, seriously, Gail." She playfully slaps me on the knee. "What would you do?"

"God, I hope it would never happen."

"Well . . ."—she takes a sip of her coffee—"you are avoiding the question."

"I'm not avoiding." I lightly scratch the lower part of my jaw. "Not a question of would do, it's a question of what I must do."

"And?"

"Report the incident and suffer the consequences."

"And lose everything? Your career and mine?"

"I can't believe you would want me to do anything else." I walk over to the coffee pot, pour myself a cup of coffee, and turn and look at her. "We both do have clearances you know!"

"But what if they just asked for some ole field manual that is nothing . . . unclassified."

"Small things lead to bigger things."

"And then sweetened the pot with good money?"

"Jesus, Lydia, and when you got caught, what then?" I twirl the cup in my hands, watching the coffee slosh ever so slightly. "Not only are you a traitor, but every woman in uniform who is friends with another woman becomes suspect." I put the coffee cup down. "It's hard enough in the dark, Lydia, it doesn't need to get darker."

"But isn't it true, that we become targets for that kind of espionage?"

"Anyone can be a target for espionage."

"You're right." She takes my hand and squeezes it. "We both know what we would have to do."

The lights flicker and then dims as the generator outside gives way to the main power station. It goes deadly quiet as the motor of the generator makes a last attempt to continue its dull roar. It is odd that they would kick over the lights at this time of evening. It is usually later, when it is much darker.

"Strange." Lydia turns and faces me. She takes and untangles the chain on her security badge. "Wonder why they switched over so early this evening?"

I shrug my shoulders.

In the distance there is a muffled explosion. We both run to the balcony and see the dark cloud rise above the snarl of shacks and other more permanent buildings. The flames leap toward the sky as the black smoke dissipates.

We watch as the fire trucks make their way along the crowded streets to the blackened site.

"They got the Montana BOQ," shouts a shadowy figure waving his arms about as he runs in the late dusk.

The Montana Bachelor Officer's Quarters belongs to our unit.

The telephone rings in the charge-of-quarter's area.

"It makes no sense." I sit with my head in my hands.

"It does"—she gently runs her hand over my shoulder—"to me."

"Lydia, we just made love and . . . and"—I look at her and stop.

I stand and walk toward the desk, grab my T-shirt, and slip on my cutoffs. I am like steel to a magnet; I return and sit down once more beside her.

"Gail," she touches my arm. "It's not over for God's sake, I just need time."

The aircraft descends into Danang. Can't see out. C123s have peepholes, but the way the web seating is built, it's impossible to look out unless you stand. It's really a cargo plane.

The motor whines, and the landing gears squeal as they are lowered. I keep thinking of SAM missiles.

The air is hot and humid. I walk out the back of the giant "guppy." Into the passenger terminal; someone is supposed to meet me here. I see Grunts everywhere; some are sleeping, others reading a book.

I turn and look in the direction of the voice. It is Lydia. I smile. I sure hope it doesn't show all over my face what I would like to do.

"Lydia, what are you doin' here?" I scratch the side of my nose. "I thought you had gone to Phu Bei."

"Heard you were comin'," she grins. "Actually waiting for a flight to Saigon."

I blush and grin, then drop my glance to the ground. Silence.

"You up for in-country R&R or assignment?" she asks.

"Assignment." I gaze off into the distance. I want to talk to her, but somehow I must make myself wait. She made it very clear.

She looks at me. She knows what I am thinking. She reaches out and lightly touches my shoulder.

"Give me time, Gail, please," she says quietly.

The noise is muffled. I hardly hear anything. The second blast is unmistakable; incoming mortar rounds. This time intelligence was accurate. I don't know where the bunkers are.

Blam! The door to my hooch flies open. What the hell do I do now? I must get under the bed. I roll off the bed slipping the mattress on top of me. I am aware of the wailing of the warning sirens. The sounds spread over me like a fire on a dry log. Sirens and the blast of each explosion. I am waiting for what? Death or an ending? So this is China Beach? I hear movement and muffled shouts—running. Blam! Sweat rolls off my forehead, running down the side of my face. I can't move.

It is quiet. It's been quiet for eons or so it seems. I hate not having any control or at least a sense of it. The all-clear sirens are sounded. I throw the mattress off. Breathe. I still don't trust the bastards. I crawl to the door. Looking outside, I see several small fires and thick smoke billowing from a JP4 fuel tank in the distance near the airfield.

I think about that plane buried in the side of Monkey Mountain—someone said it was wet and rainy; when he crashed he just stuck in the mud. All I saw was the tail of the plane. Nobody could tell me the ending. I wonder if anybody will be able to tell the ending to all of this.

It's warm and sweet smelling. I turn around and around. The drops of rain pour over my body like water from a faucet. I can hear nothing but the steady beat of the rain against the rooftop. Taking showers on the roof is a luxury. No more stench of nonpotable water. I open my mouth and take a taste of clean water, swallowing the palatable liquid.

No helicopters flying overhead. I can see my hand stretched out in front of me. Moving my hand back and forth, thankful that I had not found the bunkers at China Beach. The first incoming round had hit the bunker killing six soldiers.

My mind drifts from the horror. Cool touches. Stiff conversation. Second thoughts. No turning back. No time to be alone. Lesbian. Shame. Undesirable. Afraid. Gone. Hate. Anger. Tears. Regret?

I quickly look around. I don't know how long I've been daydreaming. I want to stay here forever. I turn my face to the pouring rain. There is movement behind me. I twist around. The watery mist parts—it's Lydia.

"How . . . how did you know I was here?" I ask.

She says nothing. I cannot move. Breathing is no longer second nature to me. Lydia encircles me with her arms. We stand swaying back and forth, hardly moving. She has her hand on the back of my neck. It's electric and calm. The smell of her skin. The movement against my breast meeting hers. She draws spirals with her fingers at the base of my neck. There is music floating all around us. Her lips against my ear.

"I want you," she whispers.

The bar is ready. The lights are on. We actually have ice. Christmas and hot weather. Champagne to vodka. The Medford BEQ will be festive tonight. The Aussies and a few of the Korean soldiers will join us.

I have borrowed the Santa Claus suit from Colonel Thornkill. Still amazes me that we would have Santa at the orphanage. It's more for us than the kids. Lydia decided that I should play Santa Claus. We made a long list of everybody's "wants." Gags and jokes. Some will mean nothing to anyone except those involved.

To Dorothy—a scale to weigh herself every morning—the dieter

To Carolyn—a bottle of Metuese wine

To Pinky—an Indian headdress

To John—a one-way ticket to Sidney

To Terry—a sterling silver stop sign

To Betty—jewelry from Thailand with customs paid in full

To Clara—a new blues guitar

To Wang Cho—hot sauce for his snakes plus a book of snake recipes

To Bill—Earplugs and a movie screen for when it rains on the roof

To everyone—a popcorn popper for movie night

To Mama-San—10 mpc for not stealing mine that I left in my pocket

To Lydia—a towel

To Lucky—a deck of cards

To me—a shower cap

"Gail," the soft insistent voice floats between darkness and reality.

"Hmmm?" I stir. My thoughts are foggy. My head feels a lot like it has grown teeth overnight.

"It's Christmas," she whispers. "We got to go to work." She runs her hand over the bottom of my foot.

I throw back the cover. I roll my body over the side of the bed, leaving my head lie on the pillow. "Oh God." I grab my head between my hands. "If I lift my head, I'll break my neck."

"Shit!" I lift my head with a jerk. The room momentarily dips, blurs, and then refocuses. "What time is it?"

"Six," answers Lydia. She throws me a cool wet washcloth.

"In the morning?" I ask. She nods. She slips her hand on the lock of my door and walks toward me. She pulls me toward her; my head rests against her chest and the OD Green T-shirt. The security badge lightly rustles as I turn my face to bury in her softness. She kisses me silently on my forehead.

"Merry Christmas."

"Merry Christmas." I smile. Pulling back, I say, "I got to get this Santa suit to work. Somebody wants to borrow it."

She brushes the hair away. "God, you look awful." She winks.

"No shit, Sherlock." I roll my eyes in my head. "If I look as awful as I feel, I gotta to die to get better." I shake my head and immediately regret it. "I should know better than to drink anything, let alone mix beer and champagne."

I pull Lydia toward me as the taxi pulls up beside us. Opening the door I hand the driver a note with the address.

"One hundred fifty," he says.

I shake my head.

"One hundred," I bargain.

"One hundred fifty."

I start to close the door.

"Okay, okay. One hundred." He throws up his hands. "You pay now." I give him the money.

The little blue-and-yellow French-made car spews black smoke as we pull out into the road. Lydia and I sitting in the back watch as the street passes beneath us. The floorboard, long rotted out, forces us to place our feet on the partially rusty frame of the little auto. We dodge in and out of the never-ending flow of people and vehicles. Endless rows of makeshift shacks become denser as we make our way deeper into the residential areas.

"Do you have any idea where we are going?" I question Lydia.

She shakes her head. "Nope."

The taxi driver pulls off to the side of the road. In front of us is a narrow walk street that looks like a long ribbon with no end. On each side of the street are small houses side by side. The street on both sides slopes to a large V-shaped gutter carrying waste products in a trickling like stream. On its way to the Saigon River.

"I go no more," he states, "You walk from here. Go down street maybe ten minutes."

Lydia and I look at each other. We get out of the taxi. The blue smoke surrounds us in a momentary cloud making us cough.

Kids come from everywhere. They cautiously hug the wall and follow us with those dark, dark eyes. One little girl breaks from the others, runs toward us, and pulls the hair on Lydia's arm. She giggles and runs back.

"Kids really are the same everywhere." Lydia looks around. "Aren't they?" She squats down and takes a package of gum, pulls out a stick, unwraps it, and puts it in her mouth. She begins to chew. She holds out a stick. One little boy shakes his head, hesitates, and then shakes his head again. Several take a stick, but no one chews it. They take it and stick it in their pocket.

"But they are different."

We walk down the crowded street; the children follow us. Some walk beside us, others move along the houses. It is quiet, very quiet. It is an uneasy quiet.

Lydia points to a house. We have reached our destination. I knock.

The hanging beads part, and my mama-san bows deeply, stands, and beckons us with her hand to follow her. As we enter, we see on the floor a table with several people sitting. They bow ever so slightly. In the middle of the table, out of place, is a small artificial Christmas tree with three blinking lights.

The silence is broken as everyone at the table says in unison, "Merrily Clistmas!"

Lydia and I are standing side by side. I take her hand and squeeze it. We both bow in our very awkward manner.

"Thank you," we say to them.

I sit waiting for customs check. The window to the flight line has a thick coat of smoke covering it. In the distance, I see an Airman chasing a dog from the tarmac airstrip. The belly of a C123 is cracked wide-open waiting for some unknown cargo. Lydia had left three months earlier, and I am anxious to get home.

I flip over the sheet of paper given to me as I came into the waiting area: *So You're Going Home.* It outlines for all "returnees" some of the things we should expect, some precautions we should take. My eyes scan the paper and come to rest at the bottom.

> *To avoid unnecessary harassment,*
> *we suggest all returnees wear civilian*
> *clothes home or change at your destination*
> *as soon as possible.*

"Group 4," comes the announcement over the PA System, "proceed to the customs counter."

I pick up my belongings and proceed to the designated area. I put my suitcase on the counter. A military police customs specialist begins rifling through my belongings, opening all containers.

"Any contraband?" he asks routinely.

I shake my head.

Pointing his finger with his arm extended he tells me to go to inspection booth A.

Once inside the inspection booth, two female MP customs inspectors tell me to strip down to pants and bra. I do. They perform the body search with practiced ease.

I dress and proceed outside the booth. My luggage has been moved to the baggage holding area and the customs clerk gives me my leave paper stamped "cleared."

I move out of the building toward the aircraft—the Big Bird—that will take us home: **Continental Airways** in bright red letters looms before me. Once inside I make my way toward my assigned seat. It's an aisle seat.

The plane slowly lifts off; loud shouts and whistles echo throughout the aircraft.

I drum my fingers against the arm of the chair. Waiting, waiting for my call to come through. The USO Lounge is crowded with people occupying time or making phone calls. The bitter coffee taste lingers in my mouth. There are three more people before me. I stand and stretch debating to get a Coke. If I move, I know I'll lose my seat. I am too nervous to sit here, need to move around. I walk over to the hostess and get a small cup of coke, the ice long melted.

I have buried myself in my room for the past three weeks, going only to work and back. Afraid to cross the street, I go to the compound a half hour earlier than I have the whole year I have been here. Everybody says that happens; you start to worry about "getting it" just before DEROS time. If not by a stray round or mortar, being hit by a truck or moped or something. The jitters about staying alive. Worrying about going home in a body bag and a box at the last minute. Doesn't matter if you were a Grunt or a Saigon Warrior—you still worry.

"Staff Sergeant Westbrook" comes a voice. I look toward the "Calls to Home" counter. The young woman nods at me. "Your call is being placed; telephone no. 4."

I rush to the booth. I pick up the telephone. The operator tells me my number is ringing.

"Hello?" comes the sleepy voice.

"Lydia!" I shout hoping she can hear me.

"Hello?" the voice a little more insistent and a little louder.

"One moment please," the operator cuts in. Silence. "Try again," I hear her say.

"Lydia?" I shout "Can you hear me?"

"Gail?" comes her voice, "Is that you, Gail?"

"Lydia, haven't got much time." I try to rush. "I'll be at Travis on Thursday. Can you be there?

"Gail, I can't . . ." The Goddamn line goes dead.

"Operator! Operator!" I shout in anger, banging on the receiver.

"I'm sorry, but there is a problem with the line" comes the operator. "Please place your call later." The line goes. Silence once again.

As the plane banks and begins to climb once again, I lean back in my seat adding endings to Lydia's unfinished conversation. We have a stopover in Hawaii and Guam. In sixteen hours or so I should know.

CHAPTER 10

The Return

The plane circles and banks making lazy circles in the sky; stacked, waiting for clearance to land. Down below, the sprawling runways of Travis Air Force Base wait for us to land. Our Silver Bird has brought all of us home—home at last.

The plane straightens up and begins the steep descent toward the landing strip. My hands are sweating. Dropping and then with a loud bang, the plane touches the ground, bounces up, the engines rev, the plane begins to ascend then floats, and finally touches the runway.

A thunderous roar fills the plane as we all shout.

Taxing toward the terminal the captain speaks over the intercom. "Second landing was better. Welcome home!"

The voice of the flight liaison officer reminds us to change into civilian clothes before going out in public. He cautions us not to talk about where we've been. Don't talk to the civilians about being in Vietnam.

I grab my briefcase and make my way off the plane. No customs; we cleared that in Hawaii. I half run and walk through the terminal. Looking in every direction. I run outside. No one. I'll go get my luggage first. I glance back in one last hopeful look. Nope.

"Hey!"

Lydia is standing directly in front of me. I drop everything and grab her in my arms. I'm burning to kiss her. We rock back and forth in a long loving hug. Silence.

"Let's get outta here," she whispers in my ear. I don't let go. I hug and hug her. She gently pushes me away.

"Let's get your luggage and get the hell outta here!" she repeats.

Words are useless. I cannot speak. I take the back of my hand and push back the tears from eyes.

In silence we get my luggage and make our way to her car.

Driving down the freeway toward Sacramento, I jump into the backseat, scramble out of my uniform into slacks and pullover. I sit back and look at Lydia through the mirror. She sees me looking at her and smiles.

I lean forward and reach around, my chin on the back of the driver's seat. The smell of her fills my senses. Tracing the outline of her body, I touch the swell of her breast. She takes a deep breath.

"Oh Jesus, Gail," she sighs.

"I'm . . . sorry. No . . . no I'm not!" I lean back in the seat. "That was unfair of me though."

She walks from the bathroom toward me, a hazy mist rolls out from under the door and almost follows her. The bath towel wrapped tightly around her falls to the floor as she loosens the fold. Standing I watch her, unable to move . . . no, not wanting to move. She takes a sharp turn and walks to the ottoman, steps up and once more faces me, her naked form like a statue on a pedestal. Wanting and needing twist and turn inside of me as I move toward her. She reaches out and gathers my head to her, and I bury my face in the warm flesh.

"*Hold me,*" she whispers.

I grab her tightly around her buttocks, and she moves her legs around me and holds my head to her breast. I feel her mons against my stomach and the wetness as her legs spread wider apart.

She takes my face in her hands and at first skims my lips with her tongue. I open my mouth and take her tongue, caress it with mine. My arms slip underneath her more as she squeezes my waist with her legs. My splayed hands sketch the roundness of her as I slowly trace my way toward her very center. She moves up on me, positioning herself for me to enter her. I stroke and caress her drawing tiny circles with my fingers.

"Oh God, Gail . . . go inside," she gasps, "Go inside!"

My breathing comes in short pants as I enter her. It's like touching the inside of an iris heavy laden with pollen: silky. I feel her tighten around my fingers as I move them farther into her.

She comes in a rush. Arching as she flows and flows over my hand and down my stomach. My knees weak, I move toward the bed, sitting on the edge. Lydia's legs are wrapped around me. Her head is leaning on my shoulder.

"Stay," she gently commands, "Stay inside me . . . don't go!"

*   *   *

I bolt up in bed, feeling as if a scream has just left me. Frantically searching for a reference point, my eyes dart around the room. Where in the hell am I? I squeeze my eyes shut. A chill passes over me as I realize that I am covered with sweat. I open first one eye and then the other. I am here with Lydia. I hold my breath and listen; her breathing in quiet rhythms soothes as I count them at regular intervals. I get up and look at Lydia lying there. I grab my head between my two hands like a vise hoping to squeeze out fragmented thoughts.

I walk over to the window and open the drapes just a crack. I'm taken back by what I see; I still expect to see concertina wire coiled around a fenced in compound. I should be there, lying beside her, forgetting everything; but I can't stop thinking. I look at the night table. The cartons of milk are half-empty— real milk. The other two cartons are in the trash basket.

I look back where she is lying. She moves. "Gail?" comes the throaty sound as her hand searches for me beside her.

"Here, by the window."

"You okay?"

"Yeah. I'm still on 'nam time I guess." I turn back toward the window. "Lydia?" Silence. I sense her waiting for my question. "How . . . how was it for you coming back? . . . I mean mentally."

I hear her sit up in bed. "Jesus! That's a heavy question at"—yawning, she stretches and grabs the watch, puts it up to the faint light coming through the window. "At four in the morning."

I hear her footsteps as she comes toward me. I feel her body as she presses close to me. Her warm breast against my back causes a rush of desire. She reaches around me, resting her chin on my shoulder. She nuzzles her cheek against my neck.

"Sweetie, it's different," she clears her throat. "Before I went over there I didn't think much about the politics of war."

"Meaning?" I revel in the feel of her, but anger's cold fingers pull me away.

"Meaning, now I do. What did we accomplish? Lot of people died. We alienate ourselves with each other." She moves her arms up and down mine as if to warm me up. "All those protesters hate the government but take it out on the warriors."

"Lydia, it's angry here, isn't it?" She turns me around slowly. She leans against me, our bodies touching from the waist down. Her hands cup my face.

She nods. "In a different sort of way." She kisses me, kindling fire. "But here, right now, it's not."

She leads me back to bed. Were we talking? The cool sheets heighten the contrast of her hot searching hands; nothing left to talk about!

Our luggage packed and the motel bill paid, we carefully turn the corner and proceed down the long stretch of road. Lydia rolls down the window. The wind blows warm through the car.

"Seems so strange."

"What?" she asks glancing in my direction.

"Seeing all these signs in English." I scan the area. "I mean not GI English."

"Yeah, I know what you mean." Lydia smiles.

It will be a long loving drive across the states to Vermont to see her mom.

We arrived in Vermont, taking in the lush green mountains as we made way to Lydia's Mom's house. Excited and anxious to go swimming in a clear mountain swimming hole that Lydia kept close to her heart during those hot sultry days in Vietnam.

She moves out into the water naturally and smoothly, cutting the surface with only small ripples. The clear water allows me to see the slightly distorted outline of her nude body. She begins her rough, uneven strokes toward the center of the little pond.

The sheets of rain have stopped. The steam rises from the ground in great clouds of white mist. She takes her forearm and wipes it across her forehead. Small beads of sweat forming on her upper lip.

"I'd sell my soul to the devil for a dip in the swim hole at home," she blows air from her bottom lip causing the hair hanging down to jump up as if pulled by a string. "Gail, you ever been to Vermont?" she looks toward me.

"Yeah, couple of times." I nod. "But not with you."

"Maybe we'll go," she says quietly, "after this is all over."

I put the last of my clothes in a neat pile beside Lydia's. A gentle breeze causes me to form goose bumps—everywhere.

"Come on, chicken," she shouts as she treads water. "There's no one here."

I move to the edge of the water debating whether to sneak in or plunge and get the first shock over with. I take the middle road and walk briskly, sucking my breath in as the water goes higher. I look to see Lydia swimming back toward me.

Standing now with my shoulders just above the surface, I watch as Lydia's dark shadow moves closer to me as she swims under water. Quietly her head breaks the surface. She sees me looking back and forth as if searching for some unknown assailant.

Reaching for me, she whispers, "We really are alone."

Her mouth is just above the water line. Ever closer, her hands at my waist, she moves her lips along the skin just above my breast where water meets shoulder. She presses her body against mine as she stands and traces my neck to my lips with the tip of her tongue. It's a new sensation, this feeling of bare skin and water. Our mouths meet slightly parted, each tongue searching, finding, and skimming the tender hot surface of the other. Desire shoots from my groin and twists and turns my stomach as it moves upward to that focal point of her tongue plunging into my mouth. My arms move around her. The water is warmer than before. It smoothes her skin, and my hands glide across her back. I pull her closer.

CHAPTER 11

Echoes

What seems like years later, I walk down the long hallway of the VA hospital. The smells fill my nose, and my gut reaction is to gag. I swallow to control my reflex. The nurses' station looms before me. Lydia was transferred yesterday from the St. Johnsbury Hospital. I keep telling myself at least she's alive.

We need some gas. Lydia signals and pulls the car off to the filling station. I look across the street and see a little store with an ice cream sign swinging in the breeze.

"Want some ice cream?" I ask.

"With real milk," she smiles. "Sure. I buy you fly." She tosses me some money.

Getting out of the car, I dodge a kid on a motorcycle recklessly doing circles in the gas station yard and head across the street. I see the top of Lydia's full head of hair bounce behind the car as she makes her way to fill the tank with gas.

I stop at the nurses' station. I turn around. I begin to pace back and forth. Returning. Going away. A nurse sitting behind the station looks up.

"May I help you?" she asks quietly.

I shake my head.

"Just waiting," I lie. I turn and head toward a chair. I sit. Taking a deep breath, I lean back.

I stand once more and go to the nurses' station. The nurse looks at me and smiles.

"You're not waiting for anyone, are you?"

I shake my head.

"I've come to see Lydia Goodman."

"Family?" She asks as she pulls out Lydia's record and opens it.

I shake my head again.

"Are you Gail?"

I nod.

"Room 112. Don't stay long. Okay?"

I turn and walk down the short distance to her room. Quietly opening the door looking toward her bed, I can see she is sleeping. I go to the chair beside her. She looks so peaceful. Her arm in a cast lies haphazardly across her body. Her thick dark hair surrounds the bandage on the right side of her head. Bald spots where the hair has been shaven are peeking through. The tent like structure over her legs remind me of . . . her legs had to be amputated just above the knees.

I give the man $1.50 for the two ice creams and head out the door. I start across the street. Looking left for traffic, I hear the motorcycle at the gas station.

Looking right. Lydia is coming out the door. Motorcycle. Wheels going round and round. Scream. Motorcycle. Smell of rubber. Sliding everything. Bounces. Lydia's arms flailing. Upside down. Disappears behind car. RUN, RUN, RUN!! Miles away can't get there. People everywhere. Let me through. Sirens. People shouting . . . Lydia! Red motorcycle, red, red everywhere. My elbow; the bastard holding me. I run. Lydia sitting funny against/between gas pumps. Her face is red. Motorcycle on her. GET THE FUCKING THING OFF!!

"Lydia, Lydia!" I yell. Can't get to her. Crawl. Grass. On my knees. "Don't Jesus fucking Christ look Lydia." Where are those fucking kids? Get my bearings got to look. Getting dark. Can't see.

Lydia takes my hand. Her eyes focus on me, and she tries to smile.

"Hi."

"Hold me," she says.

I rise and cradle her head in my arms. Her cheek is against my breast. I'm scared—scared I'll hurt her. She cries softly and I with her. I bend down and lightly kiss her forehead.

The nurse enters the room. She glances in my direction. "You'll have to leave now."

"Let her stay," Lydia quietly commands the nurse. I startle at her resolve.

"Till she falls asleep," the nurse says walking out the room.

I hold her hand throughout the night.

Light from the hallway streams through the cracked door. The nurse walks in and motions for me to follow her.

"You can sleep over there," she whispers.

"Gail." comes the whisper. "Gail."

The voice awakens me slowly. I look through the haze. It's the nurse from the station. I yawn. Sitting up, I rub my eyes and yawn again. The morning sun, coming in through the window, is so bright; I squint. Lydia's mom is coming down the hallway. Lydia's mom? I do a double take. What is she doing here so early?

A gentle hand touches my shoulder. "Gail . . . I'm sorry." It's the nurse again.

"Sorry for what?" I ask still in a sleepy fog.

Sorry. Lydia's mom. Oh God! Something is wrong with Lydia.

I look toward the door of her room. Urgently I turn toward the nurse.

"Lydia! What's the matter with Lydia? Is she okay? I got to go there." I start to run toward her room. "Why in the hell didn't you wake me?"

"STOP! She's not there."

I stumble to a clumsy halt. I spin around, glaring. I swallow hard.

"She's gone, Gail. Blood clot. In her lungs."

"NOOOOOOOOOOOOOOOOOOOOO!" I hear myself screaming. I'm falling in a deep void.

* * *

Taps echo in the bright Vermont afternoon. This is not real. Oh Jesus fucking stinking Christ! Why wasn't it me?

The last note sounds. I close my eyes, filled to the edge with tears. There is a taste of salt. I feel a hand in mine. I open my eyes. It's Lydia's mom. We embrace, both shaking as we weep. She pulls back and walks away.

I walk to the edge of her grave with dirt in my hand. I drop it back to the ground. I cannot do it. Throw the dirt down there, Down there with her. I drop to my knees and put my face in my hands and cry and cry and cry.

"I'll be back," I say half-heartedly. Lydia's mom gives me an extra squeeze. We both are trying to hide the tears. We both expect her to walk out of the house and join us.

"Oh, Gail," tears start to flow down her face. "I was scared . . . scared to death when she told me she volunteered."

She swallows hard and wipes the tears away with her fingers. "I just knew she would die . . . over there."

Why the fuck is she talking about this now when I am getting ready to leave? We sat for hours in that Goddamn house just staring instead of talking about her and how she died.

The bus appears over the rise. I pick up my suitcase. Look at Mrs. Goodman and whisper, "That's the irony of it all."

The curves in the road make my head rock back and forth as the bus swerves and sways. My friend Annie told me she would pick me up at the bus station in Springfield. I don't have to report to Fort Devens until Monday. I hope I can sleep tonight.

The hazy surrealistic state between sleep and awareness swirls and takes over.

In the far distance, his profile seems only a black line against the horizon. He approaches ever more slowly. The heat from the pavement makes his looming figure shimmer giving him an almost ghostly appearance.

My vision is telescopic, unreal. I reach down beside me and caress the smooth warm wood of the bat. I grasp and ungrasp the handle lifting it and bouncing it on the sidewalk. In the other hand, I hold the ice cream cone, twirling it around, licking it before it melts any further. I bite into it, savoring the pistachio flavor. I lean the bat against the wall. I look once again toward him. The colors are becoming more apparent. I can clearly see the red of his motorcycle.

The ice cream cone finished. I wipe my hands on the front of my jeans. I grasp the bat with both hands. I can hear the sound of his motorcycle as he gears down. I step behind the corner of the building. I feel/hear the pounding of my heart as he comes closer and closer. I take the stance of a batter, cock the bat in perfect form over my shoulder.

He rounds the corner. I swing the bat in exact timing.
"For Lydia, YOU MOTHERFUCKER!"
Bat and head collide.

A Kleenex dangles before my eyes.

"Huh?" I ask. Puzzled by the gesture, the dream staggers me.

"For the tears," the strange woman places her finger on her cheek.

"A . . . ah oh yeah thanks." I take the Kleenex. "A . . . ah this cold makes my eyes water."

She nods and looks away. "Traveling far?" she asks.

"Springfield," I reply.

Each time I take a breath, the fluids rattle. Taking in the air is hard, but it is a fight to get it back out. I walk into the emergency room waiting area. There are several people sitting, some with their head in their hands. I approach the desk.

A corpsman looks up, grabs a blank piece of paper, and proceeds to write. He reaches for a Kleenex, blows his nose, and tosses the used tissue into the basket.

"You gotta an ID?" he asks as he reaches out his hand. I give him my card. "What's your problem?"

"Having problems breathing," I wheeze.

"Have a seat." He points and hands me my ID card. "Someone will call you when the doctor is ready."

I walk to the seat and sit down toward the front of the seat. I can't sit back. It's like squeezing my lungs together. I concentrate on relaxing as I struggle with each breath. I finally stand and walk to the back of the room pausing several times to breath. An hour passes by. The room is almost empty. I feel lightheaded, and breathing is not an involuntary function. In between coughing, which has gotten progressively worse, I concentrate on the act of breathing itself.

I make my way to the desk. The corpsman looks at me with a scowl.

"I told you we'd call you."

I slam my open hand on the counter. Shaking my head, I gasp in anger.

"Can't breath, damn it," I clutch my chest. "Doctor now!" I bend forward placing my hands on my knees saying over and over to myself. In, out, in, out.

Movement and loud voices, bright lights. Sense of falling. Sounds fading and growing louder.

I count the clicks on the machine and watch the indicator needle move back down to zero as I exhale. The cycle starts once more with each deep breath I begin to take. I can feel the misty liquid enter my lungs as I slowly inhale. Last treatment today, so says the doc. I can go home.

I run toward the car blindly trying to get the door open. Fuckin' hands won't function. Nothing functions right. I slide in the seat and start the motor. Slamming the car in first gear, I move out into the street.

Crazy son-of-a-bitch squealing ties. Ahead of me coming down the street a motorcycle comes toward me. A red one. I push harder on the gas pedal. He comes closer. Everything fades away. It's just him and me. I steer the car toward the center of the road; slowly he comes closer. I steer to the other side of the road.

I slam on the brakes and car goes into a side skid. It rocks to a dangerous halt. My arms are folded over the steering wheel, my head resting on my arms. I look up. Beside me within a few inches of the car is a huge oak tree. There is no one else around. The street is quiet. I can't open the door fast enough as I begin to vomit.

"Shit, Lydia," I whisper out loud, "I don't even know what kind of flowers you like." I twirl a handful of cut flower in my hand, then lay them down.

The mound of dirt still protrudes above the level ground. The grass has taken seed, and her grave is almost green. The headstone still hasn't arrived; a simple stake with a metal-framed card marks the grave.

I take her dog tags in my hand, starting to take the chain over her head.

"Did they ever tell you why one dog tag is notched?" I ask as I stop and twist them in my hands.

She shakes her head.

"If you get killed during fighting, the notched dog tag goes between the front teeth. I put my thumb on the bottom of my upper teeth. "The other one is used for accountability."

"You're kidding me?" she backs off from me.

"I don't know if it's the truth," I say lifting the dog tags away from her. "But, sure hope to hell I never have to test that information."

I yawn and shake my head trying to rid myself of feeling groggy. I sit on the grass and look off into the distance. Near the edge of the cemetery, close to the gate, two of the groundskeepers are digging a fresh grave. I've watched this several times over the past year; another weekend in Vermont.

"I am leaving, Lydia." I look toward her grave. "It's time to let go."

I don't want to cry. My hand wipes the tears roughly from my eyes. My chest is constricted. The tears burst out.

"I'm not coming back." I drop the words like a hot iron. "I'm leaving for Alabama in a couple of weeks."

Beside me a squirrel scampers up a tree, a large acorn stuffed in his mouth. A chilly October wind blows in. I stand, brush off my slacks, and walk once again to her nameplate. I kiss my fingertips and touch her name, letting it stay there as if somehow I'm touching her.

"Good-bye, Lydia," I turn and start to walk away. Resolving I won't turn back, I keep walking. I stop; I twist around. My arms down by my side, I raise my hand from the wrist to give a distant wave. Taking a deep breath and pushing it quickly out, I proceed out of the cemetery.

Chapter 12

Drill Sergeant

We are three teams of four women. Scattered in the large bay like living quarters are pieces of gray metal sheets—unassembled wall lockers. We have been tasked with piecing together thirty of these for the bay, one for each new recruit in the platoon.

One wall locker takes 256 screws, approximately 30 minutes for each team to build. Five of us are fresh out of drill sergeant academy. The rest with the exception of Barbara are seasoned platoon sergeants not yet under the HAT. Barbara is an earlier drill sergeant academy graduate, one of the first.

The door opens. Silhouetted against the bright afternoon Alabama sun is Major Wade—Major Nellie Wade, Battalion Commander.

"At ease!" calls out Barbara. We all stop our work.

"As you were," returns Major Wade. We all make a pretense of returning to our work, but we are really watching her.

She walks down the aisle, stops at each team, watches for a while, and moves on. She goes to the door, turns, and says, "Why don't you women get your boyfriends to help you?"

She opens the door and exits without expecting an answer. The door closes. Barbara turns toward me and winks.

"We'd get more help if she'd said girlfriends."

The alarm goes off. I sit up straight. I grab the clock. Shake my head trying to focus where I am. Sorting, clicking, reaching. Friday! Oh fuck, I have flag detail. I rub my eyes. 0630! I throw the covers back and crack the Venetian blinds. My assistant drill sergeant has the troops out waiting to depart to the flagpole. I've got exactly four minutes to get out there to march them up to WAC Headquarters. Any less and we'll be late. Not only no, but hell no!!

I jump up and run to the sink and look in the mirror. Crap! I look terrible. I splash water on my face and run a brush through my hair. Good thing "the hat" hides this mop. I slap the toothbrush over my teeth. Thank God I polished my shoes before I went over to Bette's last night.

Damn! My uniform is still at her house. My others I put in the cleaners. I run to the window and peek again through the blinds. Good! They're wearing raincoats.

I look at the clock; two more minutes. I hurriedly put on bra and underpants then wiggle into panty hose. Stepping into my shoes I fasten the yellow neck scarf and pin the bottom half of the triangle to my bra. I bend down and tie my shoes.

Looking in the mirror, I put on the hat, pull the chinstrap down, and position the strap in just the right manner. Throwing on my raincoat, I start for the door as I button the last button. The belt hangs loosely down at the sides.

Opening the door, my assistant almost knocks on my nose.

She jumps back.

"Morning, Drill Sergeant Westbrook." She grins.

"Here, pleat the back of my raincoat," I command as I walk down the corridor to the barracks door, fastening the belt together.

Right on time. I face the detail and call them to attention.

"Rrrright FACE!" A two-part movement as they turn right and I turn left.

"Fooorward MARCH!" The cleats on my heels echo in the quiet morning. Rain clouds threaten in the distance. We march in silence. The troops' heads slightly turned left listening to the emphasis I automatically make when my left foot hits the pavement.

We march around the flagpole in front of the rear entrance to WAC Center Headquarters. The staff duty officer comes with the flag. Behind her is WAC center director.

Oh shit! It's a full uniform inspection. Boy, will she be in for a surprise.

I bring the detail to a halt. As I do an about-face it begins to pour rain.

I grin as the WAC center director retreats back into the building. Full uniform inspection will be another day.

Opening the door from the barracks, I see the last-minute preparations of the troops as they make themselves ready for open ranks inspection. I glance at my watch, close the door to my room, and exit out the barracks main entrance. Behind me I hear the muffled sounds of the squad leader urging the women to line up for formation.

I glance around, off to the left is Barbara exiting her barracks door. The lieutenant will be doing inspection on her platoon.

First Sergeant Kilderon walks into the room. Top-First Skirt, as we affectionately call her, fits her half lenses reading glasses on her ears, and with her head slightly bent forward, scans the room looking over the top of them.

"Is everyone here?" she asks rhetorically. We had better be. Death or duty was the only acceptable absence.

Most of us are sitting on the floor polishing our shoes, making use of every spare moment to keep up with the demands of being a drill sergeant. Others are polishing uniform insignia.

Top clears her throat. She begins to run down a shopping list of upcoming events and happenings for the week, answering questions as they come up. She reminds each of us to look at the training schedule, as there are changes.

"Battalion has asked us to inform you that effective tomorrow, no more touching troops during inspection unless you ask permission."

Everyone looks up from her shoes or brass, glance at each other, and smile.

"What's that, Top?" asks Sophie. Thank God for Sophie, she's asking the question we all wanted answered.

"You gotta ask the troops permission if you want to correct their brass or show them they have a button undone or any other gig."

"And what if they say no?" comes a quiet voice from the back. Top looks around.

"You don't touch 'em. Ya just tell 'em and it's up to them to correct it."

"Drill Sergeant Latton." Barbara looks up. "Lieutenant Brooks wants to inspect your platoon tomorrow." Barbara nods in acknowledgment.

I stand with my back to the barracks. In perfect form, I stand and take in a deep breath.

"FALL IN!" I command.

Behind me, I hear the barracks door fly open. The women move quickly into formation. First squad leader, second squad leader, third squad leader, and the fourth. Their arm extending at shoulder level straight out in front of them, automatically falling once the correct distance has been established between the squad leaders. Each successive member of the squad runs into her place, head facing to left and the right arm extended straight out from her side, assuming the position of attention once her appropriate distance has been established. The last member of each squad is turning only her head to the left aligning herself with the previous women.

Sergeant Soraday and I will be doing the inspection. Out the corner of my eye I see Barbara's platoon falling in. In the background I hear the entire company reacting to the morning of a new day.

"Ooopen ranks, MARCH! The platoon reacting to the command in four movements opens up like an accordion, allowing each access to members of each squad.

I walk to the first squad leader and look down.

"Dress and cover," I call out. Feet shuffle adjusting to the command.

Sergeant Soraday comes from the mess hall with clipboard in hand. Normally she would prepare the platoon for inspection, but this morning she had headcount for breakfast. She moves to my right as I face the first squad Leader.

The inspection begins. Like a mental list I begin the routine head-to-toe inspection:

1. Hat on straight and correctly placed with brass insignia in center
2. Proper hair length, insuring that it does not fall below the bottom line of the back collar
3. Check for makeup if used and in good taste
4. Shirt with tab correctly buttoned
5. Brass is on correctly and highly polished
6. Buttons buttoned and eagles flying
7. Name tags correctly placed and straight
8. Uniform fit
9. Is individual wearing a bra?
10. Seams on skirt correctly positioned
11. Hands positioned correctly by her side
12. Length of skirt
13. Overall cleanliness of uniform
14. Wearing nylons or pantyhose. Check to make sure they are in good repair, no runs
15. Shoes polished, in good repair and laced properly
16. Check to see if individual is assuming the proper position of attention

I call out the deficiencies and Sergeant Soraday writes them down. We both move two steps to the right and begin again. I stop at the collar. Private Babb-Williamson's brass is on crooked; I remember Top's edict.

"May I touch you?" I ask. I wait for her answer.

I can see a slight movement in her forehead. Her eyes move to look at me, breaking the position of attention. She draws in her breath.

"Where?" she whispers with a scowl on her face.

I am dumbfounded. Sergeant Soraday and I turn and look at each other and smile.

We move down the line, inspecting each person.

"May I touch you on the collar?" I hear myself say.

Her progress throughout the cycle had been steady, growing, but something was wrong. She was holding back. She had a certain sadness about her. It began when the first pass was given to the new recruits.

Pushing on the intercom button, I say, "Sergeant Soraday, send in Private Aldridge."

It was time for weekly counseling sessions. Perhaps this evening she would share with me why she had changed.

Knock! Knock!

"Enter!"

She walks toward my desk. Standing straight as a stick, she spurts, "Drill Sergeant Westbrook, Private Aldridge reporting as directed!"

Earlier I had purposely placed the chair over to the side of my desk. I motion for her to sit down. She smells of shoe polish. I look at her hands; large, gentle hands. She says nothing as she moves toward the chair. There is an uncomfortable quiet.

"Aldridge," I say, "last couple of days I've noticed—"

She cuts me short. "Cut the crap, Drill Sergeant," she spits out.

I am not prepared for this hostility. Her eyes fill with tears. She glares at me as they roll down her cheeks. Her bottom lip quivers.

"Wanna share?" I ask. Dangerous technique, it can bring problems.

"You would never understand," she says almost to herself. "Something I have to work out myself."

"Try me," I prod.

She shifts in her chair. She wipes the tears from her eyes with the back of her hand. She turns and stares out the window.

"My, ah . . . ah . . . girlfriend left me," she says rapid fire.

"Your what?"

"You heard right!" her eyes watching me closely.

"I'm sorry. That's rough." Jesus, I hope I've handled this right. This could blow up right in my face. I wait.

"I put you in a spot, didn't I?" she asks.

I nod.

"You going to report me?"

"For what?"

"Well hell . . . you know what!"

"Do you want me to?"

She shakes her head.

The knock is soft at first and then it ends with a louder thump.

"Sound off!" I call out.

"Drill Sergeant Westbrook, Private Aldridge requests permission to enter!"

"Enter!"

"She walks in and stands before my desk. I look at her somber face. Looking away, I tell her to take a seat.

I take a pack of cigarettes from the drawer, pull out a cigarette, and slowly inhale as I light it.

"I didn't know you smoked, Drill Sergeant."

"Sometimes. Not very often." I look at her once again. "What's up?"

"I . . . I keep waiting for the axe to fall," she falters avoiding the real issue.

"What axe?"

"You know . . . last week when I told you about my friend leaving me."

"And?" I snuff the cigarette out in the ashtray.

"Well, shit, Drill Sergeant. I mean excuse me. You know, about turning me in."

"Turning you in because your friend left you?"

"Well, no. For being . . . God, this is hard."

"Just think about what you say before you say it."

She sits in silence. I pull out a notebook, but I see nothing in the printed words. I shut the notebook and lay it on the desk. Picking up a pencil, I begin to draw arrows on a blank piece of paper.

"Are you a . . . too?"

"We are not talking about me." I put the pencil down, walking over to the window. "Aldridge, you made a choice when you came in, one with a certain amount of risk. You made one the other day when you told me about your friend." I look out on the barracks grounds. "I am not God. I might judge people, but I won't pass judgment. That's for someone bigger than me."

"Well, what does that have to do with turning me in?" She gives me a puzzled look.

"I didn't, and I won't provide you never put me in a situation to make that choice. It belongs to you and the person you share it with. Not me or anyone else."

She looks at me and shakes her head.

"It's the times, Aldridge. It's the rotten times."

I look in my new assistant's room, and CPL Brown is gone. I guess I'd better get the detail up to the mess hall.

"Drill Sergeant Westbrook!"

"Yes." I turn to face the young troop as she assumes the position of parade rest.

"You . . . you know that Private Pearson is gone!"

"Gone?"

"Yes, Drill Sergeant. She left with CPL Brown."

"What time?" I inquire, trying to keep the urgency masked.

"About four this morning."

"Four!" My voice booms. Private Janson flinches. "That Goddamn fool," I say under my breath.

"Beg your pardon, Drill Sergeant."

"Thanks, Janson." I quickly offer. "Form the squad and move them over to the mess hall." I glance at my watch. First Sergeant should be in. My head begins to throb.

It's Monday. I have one hell of a headache, and I am about to drop a bomb on the first sergeant. I pull a cigarette out, light it, inhale deeply; blowing the smoke through my nose, I begin the short walk across the field to see Top.

The talk about CPL Brown rushes through the cadre like fire.

I am sitting in one of the Drill Sergeant's apartment, listening, sometimes zoning out.

"Stupid bitch." She takes a long drag off her cigarette and blows it toward the open window.

"Why do you say stupid bitch?" I ask suspiciously.

"You don't fool around with trainees."

"Granted! But why stupid bitch?"

"Well, Gail," she patronizes, "any self-respecting lesbian who fools around with a trainee-e-e in the barracks is a simpleminded stupid bitch." She slams the cigarette back into her mouth.

"I don't like that word."

"What word?"

"Lesbian," I stutter. I pick up a piece of paper and begin folding and folding it in tiny squares.

"You don't what?" She throws her head back. "Ha! That's a joke considering you are one." Her eyes crinkle with laughter as she shakes her head.

"I AM NOT!" My voice rising in controlled anger. I toss the tightly folded paper in the ashtray. I grab the pack of cigarettes and take one, breaking it in half as I pull it shout. "Shit!" I lay the package down.

She looks at me. "Well, excuse me!" She folds her hands into her lap in a mock gesture of propriety. "That must have been some other woman dancing with Bette," she rolls her eyes. "I could have sworn it was you."

"Cut the crap!" I get up and walk toward the window and begin to shut it.

"Okay, okay! She throws up her hands in front of her face. "You need to look up the word and read what it says in the definition.

"I don't give a shit about the definition." I return to the window and reopen it. "It's a sleazy word. It sounds like a disease, dirty and incurable."

"In the Army," she hisses. "Jesus, they got you just where they want you."

"Meaning?" I brush my hand through my hair.

"Thinking you are sleazy. Fuck you! You're a masochist."

"You're impossible." I sigh. I fold my arms across my chest. I turn and plop down in the chair. I stand and begin a slow pace back and forth.

"Nancy, don't you get it. It's a fucking crime." I stop and whirl about. Glaring at her, I shout, "I AM NO GODDAMN CRIMINAL, and I won't be labeled one." All my life I've separated my love of women from the derogatory words in the dictionary.

She puts her hand on the back of my head and turns me toward the mirror hanging on the wall. "Well, sweetie pie, take a good long look in the mirror. Say hello to a criminal."

I spin around and throw her arm from me. I walk toward the mirror and with the palm of my hand slap it against my image. "I don't feel dirty with a woman. And I sure as hell don't want to be cured."

"You were very uncomfortable yesterday," she sighs. "Weren't you?"

"You want the truth?" I look at her.

"Of course." She nods. "I wouldn't ask if I didn't."

I stand up and walk toward the bookcase, picking up a small glass figurine. I look at it as if I could get the answer there. Setting it down, I turn and face her.

"I can sit all day and talk politics and religion, even softball." I spit. "But it irks the hell out of me to talk about my sexuality or yours or anyone's!"

"Why?" she asks.

"First of all, who gives a shit? We all know what we are—"

"Do you?" she challenges.

"Oh stop it!" I snarl. I clench my fists and cross my arms across my chest.

"No damn it, I won't stop it." She reaches for a cigarette. "You asked me if I wanted the truth . . . so spit it out!"

"Well, shit Nancy, the truth is obvious."

"To whom?" She gets up from the chair and walks toward the refrigerator.

"Nancy," I say quietly, my hands down beside me. "Let's stop this cat and mouse game. It's just putting both of us on the defense. We're friends, and there is enough stuff going on."

"Agreed." She takes her hand from the refrigerator. She puts the unlit cigarette in her mouth and lights it. Doing a shallow pull and quick exhale, she leans her butt against the small bar size refrigerator.

"I got my orders," I say quietly.

It's May. I've got another cycle of trainees just finished. The south is coming alive with summer fast approaching, and I'm trying hard not to remember Lydia.

"This Goddamn refrigerator won't . . ." I grunt to myself. I told the landlord that I would be moving out this weekend. Figured I could get it done using a series of pulleys and carts.

I push the refrigerator forward, trying to get the step dolly under it so that I can take it down the stairs. My pickup is backed up as close to the stairs as I can get it. If I can get the damn thing down the stairs, I can tip it onto the bed of the truck. With blanket underneath, I should be able to push it farther into the back end without any major problems.

"Can I help?" comes a voice with no body. I look around.

"What?"

"Can I help?" the woman says, peaking around the corner of the refrigerator.

"Private Beyer!" I say with surprise. "What in the world are you doing here?"

"Offering to help!" She smiles.

It's so unsettling to see her. She has the same deep widow's peak with dark hair that Lydia had. Her smile too produces the same kind of dimples that Lydia had. When she reported to my platoon for training, I stuttered and stammered for five minutes before I could speak coherently.

"A . . . I appreciate the offer, but a . . . a . . . your being here isn't quite right."

"Hey, Drill Sergeant," she teases." The cycle is ended. I am no longer a trainee."

"Well . . ." I stammer. "I could, oh hell what the heck. I could use the help." She smiles and right away the work gets easier.

We work without many words. Exchanging only recommendations and questions about which way to move something. It's hard work, and the temperature is rising as the day wears on.

"Hey! Let's take a break," I stop and wipe the sweat from my neck. "I got some lemonade in a thermos here."

"Great!"

"Unless you want a beer?" I look in her direction. "I'll have to go buy some."

"Lemonade is fine."

I walk and get the thermos. Coming back, I see her sitting on the steps. She is leaning with her eyes closed against the column of the porch.

The hot sultry weather weighs on me like a heavy stone. Making my way to the top of the building, I hope to find a small breeze to give some relief.

I scan the area. Empty. No, wait over in the corner by the front of the building, where the sand bags form a protective nest, is Lydia, half-sitting, half-lying, her head leaning against a stack of sand bags. Her eyes are closed.

I quietly walk toward her. She slowly opens her eyes and turns in my direction.

"Hi." She smiles.

"Hi," I say in return. "Penny for your thoughts."

It's hotter up here than down in my room. Even the cool breeze is blowing hot.

I clear my throat. Sitting down near Private Beyer, opening the thermos, I pour the lemonade in a paper cup and hand it to her.

"Thanks." She takes the cup and begins to drink.

"It's me that should say thanks, Private Beyer—"

"Can't you call me Susan?"

"I a . . . a don't know. Seems funny." I hesitate. "It's really not appropriate, considering the circumstances."

"Meaning?"

"Meaning, I was your drill sergeant. I'm an NCO, you're junior enlisted."

"I'm not staying here. I'm going to Fort Ord." Her eyes sparkle. "Lighten up, Drill Sergeant!"

"Gail." I smile back.

It is quiet. She sits down the paper cup. She takes her hand and brushes it through her hair, then with her bottom lip she blows air so that a straggling piece of hair on head jumps up. I stare directly at her. My god, it's a moment frozen in time.

"Hey!" I hear her shout. Her hands are waving in front of me.

"Huh?" I begin to focus. "Oh, excuse me." I am tongue-tied. A moment rushes by. "That gesture reminded me of someone I used to know."

"Used to?" She asks with a grin. "Don't you know her anymore?"

"She's . . . dead."

She reaches out and touches my arm. "I'm sorry," she whispers.

"Come on," I get up. "I want to finish this move before midnight." I reach out and give her my hand and pull her up.

Private Beyer—for one day, Susan—had disappeared, like so many other trainees.

CHAPTER 13

Home Again

My tour as a Drill Sergeant has ended and I received new orders. It was time to see Mom.

My hands slide in and out of my pockets as though there were grease at the opening. I dig deep and grasp a warm quarter, turning it over and over in my fingers.

The old man bends closer to the book he has opened on the desk.

"When did you say she was buried . . . what year?"

"Nineteen sixty-five," I almost whisper and then repeat it louder in case he didn't hear or I didn't speak.

His dirty finger slides down the page. The wisp of gray fuzzy hair on the back of his neck sways back and forth as the breeze slides through the open window.

"Lot 78, section 4." He slams the book closed and turns to go.

"Thanks," I call out. I thought I would never forget where Mom was buried.

I search the twists and turns of graveled road, squinting, searching for section 4. I stop. It is nothing what I remember. It is crowded. I remember it being slightly isolated.

The stone of rose-colored granite glistens in the early spring morning.

"Ya got neighbors, Mom!" I smile as I touch my hand to her name. "This time, I'm on my way to Germany. What do ya think of that?"